Ash and Frost: The

Trials of Guilt, Courage, and Self-Discovery

Serena Knight

Copyright © 2024 by Serena Knight

All rights reserved. No part of this book may be used or reproduced in any form whatsoever without written permission except in the case of brief quotations in critical articles or reviews.

First Edition: November 2024

Table of Contents

Chapter 1 Exile in Ice 1

Chapter 2 A Fire in the Snow 16

Chapter 3 Strangers and Survival 35

Chapter 4 A Mysterious Guide 52

Chapter 5 Whispers in the Shadows 72

Chapter 6 The Mountain's Maze 86

Chapter 7 Spirits of the Past 103

Chapter 8 Echoes of Regret 119

Chapter 9 Trust Forged in Frost 135

Chapter 10 Shadows of Doubt 150

Chapter 11 The Hidden Path 165

Chapter 12 The Toll of Power 180

Chapter 13 The Mountain's Judgment 194

Chapter 14 The Trial of Sacrifice 207

Chapter 15 Acceptance at the Summit.................................... 220

Epilogue A Guardian Reborn.. 234

Chapter 1
Exile in Ice

Freya's boots sank heavily into the snow, the crunch beneath them an unsteady rhythm against the vast silence. The Glacial Rift was an unforgiving place, an endless landscape of jagged ice and ghostly shadows. She clenched her fists, pulling her furs tighter against the biting wind that clawed at every exposed inch of skin. The cold felt personal, as though the mountain itself were punishing her with each step, as though it whispered accusations into her ear.

"Traitor," she muttered bitterly, her voice lost in the howling wind. Her breath hung briefly in the air, crystalline and fragile, before disappearing as if it, too, wanted to escape.

"You are not a Guardian, Freya." The council elder's voice echoed through her memory, a bitter reminder of her fall from grace. She could almost see his face—stern, unyielding, the kind that could carve cold truth into a person's soul. "You are a disgrace. You are not worthy of the title."

Freya's fingers flexed around the frost-covered spear she held, the weight of it a cold comfort. She had earned that weapon, trained tirelessly under Elder Iska's watchful eye, learned each precise movement as though her life depended on it—which, in their village, it often did. And she'd held her rank proudly. But now? She was only a ghost of the Guardian she had once been, stripped of everything familiar and abandoned in the cold to bear the burden of her failure.

"I'm not... I'm not what they say," she murmured, her voice unsteady. But even as she spoke, doubt gnawed at her, winding tightly around the thin thread of conviction she clung to.

The mountainside was steep and treacherous, forcing her to slow as she moved carefully over patches of ice. Her cloak billowed with each gust, its tattered edges a reminder of how unprepared she'd been for exile. She reached for the small charm hidden beneath her cloak—a braid of woven leather Elder Iska had given her when she'd completed her Guardian trials. She could still hear his voice, quiet and steady, as he'd placed it around her neck.

"Remember, Freya," he'd said, "this is not just a title. It is a vow. A Guardian stands for more than themselves."

His words clung to her heart even now, filling her with the hollow ache of regret. She tightened her grip on the charm, her knuckles white against the cold leather.

"Why did you believe in me?" she whispered, her voice almost a plea, swallowed by the roaring wind. "How could you look at me with such faith, only for it to end like this?"

"Because you wanted that faith, but did not understand the weight of it." The words were her own, but the voice that spoke them was harsh, unforgiving. The person she'd become after her exile.

Freya pressed on, forcing her legs to move forward, though every part of her wanted to sink into the snow and disappear, to let the mountain take her and bury the shame of her failure.

The isolation pressed in around her, growing heavier with each passing moment. She could almost feel the weight of the villagers' eyes, the judgment that clung to her like a second skin.

"Is this really what I deserve?" she asked the emptiness, her voice small against the expanse of ice. "To be cast out, left to… to become nothing?"

There was no answer, only the endless scream of the wind and the frigid emptiness that stretched before her. Heart Village was a distant memory now, a place she could barely envision through the fog of guilt that clouded her mind. She could remember flashes—Iska's calm eyes, the laughter of her fellow Guardians, the warmth of the hearth on long, winter nights. They felt like pieces of another life, shards of a world she could never return to.

"Elder Iska wouldn't want this for me," she said aloud, as though his spirit might hear her. "He wouldn't want me to give up." But even as she spoke, the doubt slithered back in, whispering questions she couldn't silence.

"Are you so sure?" the voice in her mind hissed. "After all, you're the one who let him down."

Freya swallowed, the guilt rising like bile. She took a shaky breath, willing herself to stay strong. "No. No, I won't let this be the end," she said, louder this time, her voice defiant against the oppressive silence.

The wind seemed to shift, carrying a sound she hadn't noticed before—a faint whisper, barely audible, like a memory breathed into the cold air. It was her own voice, from a time she'd nearly forgotten.

"Guardians don't run from the mountain. They conquer it."

Freya straightened, her fingers loosening their grip on the charm. "I will prove them wrong," she murmured, the conviction settling over her like armor. "I may be alone, but I won't let their judgment be my end."

With renewed resolve, she continued her climb, her breaths measured, steady.

Freya pulled her furs tighter around her shoulders as she trudged forward, each breath forming a frosty cloud that hung in the air for a fleeting moment before the wind tore it away. The cold bit into her skin, slipping through every seam, every fold, as if determined to remind her that she didn't belong here. The Glacial Rift was a place of exile, a harsh, unyielding realm where no warmth survived, where only the strong—or the foolish—dared to tread.

With each step, the cold seemed to sharpen, cutting through her resolve like a blade of ice.

"You're not going to break me," she whispered into the wind, as if the mountain could hear her. Her voice was rough, barely audible, yet the words felt like a promise.

She paused, shifting her weight as her foot sank into a patch of deep snow. Her fingers ached as she flexed them around the handle of her spear, the frost biting into her skin even through her gloves. The cold had always been her ally, her element to control and command. But out here, it felt different—hostile, unyielding, as though the mountain itself wanted her gone.

"Is that all you've got?" she muttered, a faint smirk crossing her lips as she looked up at the darkening sky, snow beginning to fall around her. "Come on, show me more."

The wind seemed to answer her, picking up strength until it howled through the jagged cliffs, whipping snow and ice into her face. It stung, sharp as needles, tearing at the exposed skin along her cheeks and brow.

Her hands tightened around the spear. "Is that how it's going to be?" She took a shaky breath, steeling herself against the storm's fury. "You're not going to scare me off, you hear?"

The wind roared in response, louder, fiercer. She could feel it testing her, pushing against her, as if daring her to press on. The mountain had no patience for weakness, no tolerance for fear. It would chew her up and bury her in its depths without a second thought. She took a step forward, then another, her gaze fixed on the distance. One foot in front of the other. That was all it took.

But with each step, the mountain's silence seemed to grow heavier, pressing down on her like a weight. Her mind drifted, wandering to memories she had tried so hard to leave behind.

"I never thought it would come to this," she murmured, almost to herself. "Heart Village feels like… another life."

She could almost see it—the narrow, winding streets, the warmth of the hearth fires glowing in every window, her fellow Guardians with their easy laughter and familiar faces. She remembered training sessions with Elder Iska, his patient voice correcting her form, his steady gaze watching her every move. She'd taken it all for granted, every moment, every lesson.

Elder Iska's voice echoed in her mind. "The cold is an extension of you, Freya. You must wield it as you would a weapon—with control, with purpose."

"What control do I have now?" she whispered bitterly, clenching her fists. "I couldn't even save you, let alone myself."

The words hung in the air, swallowed up by the relentless wind. She shook her head, as if she could shake away the guilt that clung to her. Elder Iska had trusted her, believed in her, and she had let him down. But no amount of regret would change what had happened, no amount of wishing would bring back the life she'd lost.

She took another step forward, digging her boots into the snow. "I can't let it end like this," she said, her voice stronger this time. "I didn't survive the council's judgment to fall here. I won't give them that satisfaction."

The wind seemed to push back, harder, as if in response. She could feel it biting at her, testing her, challenging her resolve.

She braced herself, pulling her furs tighter, her gaze hardening as she stared into the icy expanse ahead.

"You're going to have to try harder than that," she said, her words laced with defiance. "I'm still here."

The cold lashed out, fiercer than before, as if enraged by her determination. Snow whipped around her in violent gusts, obscuring her vision, chilling her to the bone. Every instinct screamed at her to stop, to find shelter, but she kept moving, each step a silent act of defiance.

"Do you hear me?" she shouted into the storm, her voice swallowed by the howling wind. "I'm not afraid of you!"

A wave of dizziness washed over her, her body trembling with the effort to keep moving, but she pushed through it. The cold might claim her in the end, might take her down as it had countless others, but she would not give in easily. She would endure, she would survive. She had to. It was the only way to make things right.

"Elder Iska," she murmured, her voice soft, almost reverent. "If you're watching… if there's still a chance… I'll prove myself. I'll be the Guardian you believed I could be."

The wind seemed to ease, just for a moment, as if granting her a reprieve. She stood still, catching her breath, feeling the sting of the cold recede just slightly. And in that moment, she felt something strange—a quiet strength, a spark of warmth flickering within her chest, reminding her of who she was, of who she could still be.

With one last steadying breath, Freya squared her shoulders and pressed on, her steps sure and unyielding against the endless snow.

The snow beneath Freya's boots gave way, sinking her heels deeper into the frozen ground with every step. She paused, her breath coming in sharp, shallow gasps that clouded the air. Her hand reached instinctively for the small charm around her neck—a simple braid of leather, frayed at the edges, but solid beneath her fingertips. Elder Iska had woven it himself, tying it with the same steady hands that had guided her through years of training, binding her to her purpose as a Guardian.

As she held the charm, her chest tightened, the warmth of memory threatening to unravel her resolve.

"Steady yourself, Freya," she whispered, gripping the charm until it pressed painfully into her palm. "You're stronger than this."

She closed her eyes, letting the silence around her settle as she remembered his voice, low and calm, filling the training grounds as it had so many times. "The strength of a Guardian isn't in their power," he'd told her once, his tone as gentle as the touch of a winter breeze. "It's in their discipline, their ability to rise above emotion and remain focused on their purpose."

Freya swallowed, her throat tight. "What good is discipline if you're still… still human beneath it all?" Her voice cracked, and she let out a harsh breath, the sound lost in the vast, empty silence.

As she traced the edges of the leather braid, the memory shifted, darkening, as though the very mountain wanted to remind her why she was here. She saw Elder Iska's face again, but it was not kind or steady this time; it was cold, lined with disappointment.

"Freya," his voice echoed in her mind, brittle and unforgiving. "This path you have chosen—it's a betrayal. Of all of us."

"No," she whispered, shaking her head as if she could dispel the memory. But his words clung to her, as they always did, creeping back at her weakest moments, filling her with doubt and regret. She could still feel the weight of the council's judgment, the harsh eyes that had looked down on her from the stone dais, condemning her.

"Iska…" Her voice was barely a murmur, a plea spoken to no one. "I… I didn't mean for it to happen. I thought I was—" Her words faltered, the explanation she'd rehearsed so many times feeling hollow in the face of his imagined gaze. She'd thought she was protecting them, that her actions had been justified, necessary. But she'd lost control, and the consequences had shattered everything she'd once believed about herself.

"Enough," she said firmly, squeezing the charm until the leather bit into her skin. "This self-pity won't get me anywhere. I can't change what happened."

Her fingers traced the small knot at the center of the charm, the place where Iska had tied it. She remembered his words that day as if he were beside her. "No matter what you face, remember this: you carry our legacy within you, a legacy that must be protected, upheld. The mountain will test you, but you must be unbreakable, Freya."

The words struck her now with the weight of irony, heavy and bitter. How could she uphold any legacy when she'd been cast out, branded a traitor by the very people who had once trusted her most?

"Unbreakable," she whispered, the word foreign and cold on her tongue. "If only it were that simple." She closed her eyes, trying to draw strength from the memory of his belief in her, even if it had faded, leaving only remnants of who she used to be.

A sharp gust of wind cut through her cloak, pulling her out of her reverie. She blinked, squaring her shoulders, forcing her hands to her sides. "No. This isn't who I am anymore," she said quietly, as if saying it aloud would somehow make it true.

She looked out at the vast stretch of snow, the endless white that seemed to swallow her up. "Survival first," she reminded herself, her voice hardening with each word. "Redemption comes after. If I want to make things right, if I want them to see I'm more than my mistakes… I have to survive."

But doubt lingered, stubborn as the cold. "What if there's nothing left to prove?" a small voice inside her whispered. "What if surviving doesn't change anything?"

Freya clenched her fists, driving her nails into her palms. "Then I'll change it," she answered fiercely. "One step, one breath. I'll make them see who I truly am, or I'll die trying."

With a final look at the charm, she tucked it back beneath her cloak, letting its weight press against her heart as a reminder— a tether to a past that still held pieces of herself, pieces she could reclaim. She set her jaw, her gaze hardening as she turned toward the path ahead.

"Watch me, Iska," she murmured, her voice as cold and steady as the wind that whipped around her. "I may have failed before, but this time... I won't fall."

As she took her first step forward, the mountain loomed, indifferent yet waiting, as though challenging her words. And Freya, feeling the ache of guilt finally give way to the steel of determination, met its silent dare head-on.

The sky was sinking into shades of deep indigo, casting long, eerie shadows across the snowy expanse. Freya paused, glancing back at the trail she'd carved through the drifts, the line of her footprints already softening under the wind's relentless touch. Darkness settled around her like a heavy cloak, pressing down with a chill that sank deep into her bones.

"Feels like you're watching me, doesn't it?" she murmured, her voice barely louder than a whisper.

There was no answer, of course—just the haunting silence of the mountain and the distant echo of the wind curling through crevices and crags. And yet, it was there, that feeling, as if something ancient and unseen observed her, a quiet judgment hovering over every step she took.

Freya shook her head, trying to dispel the sensation, but it clung to her, a subtle weight, prickling at her nerves.

"Freya," she muttered, chiding herself. "You're letting the cold get to your head."

But the stillness only deepened, thick and watchful. She took a slow breath, exhaling in a frosty cloud that hung in the air, lingering longer than it should, as though even her breath resisted the silence around her. She clutched her cloak tighter, unable to shake the notion that she wasn't truly alone.

"Is this what you wanted?" she asked the darkness, her voice a low, bitter sound. "For me to wander through the snow until there's nothing left?"

The wind shifted, rustling through the surrounding ice like an answer, and she could almost hear words within it—words filled with disappointment, resentment. She imagined voices from the village, echoing their judgment, whispers seeping into her thoughts.

"You   betrayed   us."
"You broke the code, Freya. Guardians don't act on impulse."
"You don't belong."

Freya clenched her fists, shaking her head fiercely. "No. I'm more than that. I'm more than—"

The wind rose sharply, drowning her voice with a fierce, biting howl. She staggered back, bracing against the onslaught, her heart pounding as though the mountain itself were responding, rebuking her defiance.

"Oh, so you do hear me," she called out, her voice trembling slightly, but laced with anger. "Or maybe I'm just losing my mind. That's what you want, isn't it? To break me down until I'm nothing more than one of your ghosts?"

The wind fell abruptly, leaving an intense, echoing silence. She felt her heart hammer in the stillness, as though she'd just crossed an invisible line, the atmosphere thickening with an almost tangible sense of anticipation.

"Is that it?" she whispered, squinting into the shadowy stretches of snow and rock. "You're waiting for me to… what, to prove something? To collapse? To beg?" She laughed, a hollow, humorless sound. "You'll have to wait a while, then. Because I won't be broken that easily."

Yet the silence persisted, deepening, shifting around her like a presence, a force that pressed against her skin, as if the mountain itself understood her defiance. She shivered, though it was not the cold that chilled her now, but a sense of something vast and unknowable, bearing down upon her with a judgment older than any she'd ever known.

She drew in a shaky breath, her voice soft. "Fine, then. If you have something to say, then say it. Show me what you really want from me."

The shadows seemed to stir, a darkness pooling at the edge of her vision, gathering into strange shapes, jagged and formless, shifting like smoke caught in an invisible breeze. For a moment, she thought she saw eyes within the darkness—cold, indifferent, gazing at her with a judgment she couldn't quite grasp.

"You want to test me?" she said, her voice low, almost daring. "Is that it? Go on, then. I'm still standing. I'm still here."

The silence around her thickened, pressing in until it felt like it might crush her. She found herself staring into the shadows, the darkness seeping into every corner of her mind, filling it with whispers that weren't quite words, but meanings, accusations, memories.

"Freya…"

The sound was soft, almost inaudible, like a memory breathed into life. She stiffened, her grip tightening around her cloak.

"Who's there?" she demanded, her voice barely steady.

The darkness shifted, a flicker of movement just beyond her vision, and for an instant, she thought she saw a familiar face—

a face lined with age and wisdom, with eyes that had once looked upon her with kindness.

"Iska?" she breathed, feeling the name tremble on her lips, a flicker of something raw and painful beneath it.

The face was gone, swallowed by the shadows, leaving only the lingering sense of loss, the ache of a presence that had long since faded.

"No," she whispered, shaking her head, as if she could shake off the memory. "This is just… the cold. The isolation. I'm alone." She tried to force herself to believe it, to ignore the feeling that hung over her, the watchful, waiting gaze.

But even as she pressed on, her steps slow and wary, she could feel it—that quiet, unseen presence, lingering in every shadow, whispering of trials yet to come, of pain yet unspoken. She swallowed hard, each step heavier than the last, her body tense, as though bracing for a blow that had yet to fall.

"Whatever you are, whatever you're trying to show me," she murmured, her voice barely a breath against the chill, "I'll face it. I'll face it all."

And with those words, she moved forward into the darkness, feeling the mountain's gaze upon her, knowing that whatever lay ahead would be unlike anything she'd ever faced before.

Chapter 2
A Fire in the Snow

Freya's boots crunched through the snow as she pressed on, her eyes squinting against the harsh reflection of sunlight off the ice. The silence of the mountains was thick, unbroken, except for the occasional gust of wind that stirred the snow into twisting flurries around her. She kept her focus forward, her thoughts distant, fixed on surviving another day in this merciless expanse.

Then, something caught her eye—a dark shape, half-buried in a drift just a few paces off her path. Freya froze, instinctively tightening her grip on her spear, her gaze sharp and cautious. She approached slowly, heart pounding, her every sense alert.

As she drew closer, the shape took form: a man, lying prone, almost completely covered by snow. His cloak was dusted with frost, the edges stiff and cracked, and she could see the shallow rise and fall of his breath. He was alive—barely.

Freya's eyes narrowed, her gaze sweeping over him, assessing. There was something familiar about his attire—the heavy, blackened leathers, the intricate, flame-like patterns etched into his cloak. Her stomach tightened as her gaze settled on the emblem stitched into his sleeve: a flame crest, bold and unmistakable.

"A Firelander," she muttered, voice barely more than a breath. She took a step back, the spear shifting in her hand. Her instincts screamed at her to leave him. The history between their people was bloody and long. Firelanders and the Icefolk had been enemies for as long as she could remember, their alliances fraught with betrayal and violence. This man, whoever he was, wasn't her concern. She had no reason to help him.

And yet… she lingered, her gaze lingering on the harsh lines of his face, barely visible beneath his cloak. The rise and fall of his chest was weak, unsteady. Abandoning him would mean his death. But helping him… that could mean trouble she didn't need.

Freya scowled, muttering to herself, "Why did you have to be here? Why now, of all times?" She hesitated, torn between her instincts and something deeper—something she didn't want to acknowledge.

With a frustrated sigh, she dropped to one knee, nudging his shoulder. "Hey," she called, her voice low, cautious. "Can you hear me?"

The man didn't stir, his breath still faint and shallow. Freya gritted her teeth, knowing she was wasting precious time. She leaned in closer, trying to rouse him with another gentle shake. "Come on," she muttered, louder this time. "Wake up. I don't have all day."

To her surprise, his eyes fluttered, a hint of awareness breaking through the haze. His gaze was unfocused, slipping past her before settling, sluggishly, on her face. He blinked, confusion flickering in his dark eyes.

"What…?" His voice was rough, barely audible, the sound scraping against the cold air.

"You're lucky I found you," Freya said, keeping her tone flat. "Or unlucky, depending on how you see it."

His brow furrowed, confusion mingling with a hint of wariness. "Who… are you?"

"Someone who doesn't make a habit of saving strangers," she replied curtly. "Especially not Firelanders."

At the word 'Firelander,' something flickered in his gaze—a recognition, followed by a flash of defiance, though his strength was clearly waning. "And I don't make a habit of being… saved by Icefolk," he retorted, his voice barely a rasp.

Freya arched a brow, unimpressed. "Suit yourself. I can leave you here if you'd rather freeze."

He didn't answer, his eyes slipping shut again, as if even the effort of speaking had drained him. Freya huffed, glancing around. The temperature was dropping fast, and leaving him here would mean certain death. She let out a frustrated sigh, muttering under her breath, "Elder Iska would call this foolish."

With one last look at his still form, she muttered, "Fine. But only because I don't have the heart to leave you to the mountain. Don't make me regret it."

She hooked her arms under his shoulders, bracing herself before she started to drag him through the snow. Her muscles strained against his weight, and every step was a challenge against the cold and the rough terrain. Despite herself, she spoke aloud as she pulled him along, as if the sound might keep her going.

"You Firelanders have a knack for trouble, don't you?" she grumbled, her breath clouding in the air as she spoke. "Of all places, you end up here. What were you even doing in the Glacial Rift?"

He didn't respond, of course, too far gone to hear her questions, but she found herself filling the silence anyway.

"It doesn't matter," she said, half to herself. "It's not like you'll tell me willingly." She paused, readjusting her grip and muttering under her breath. "Just don't expect any favors once you wake up."

They reached a small overhang, sheltered enough to block most of the wind. Freya set him down as gently as her patience allowed, propping him against the icy wall of the alcove. She shook his shoulder again, trying to rouse him one last time.

"Hey," she said, a bit louder. "If you're going to survive the night, you're going to need to help yourself. I can't carry you forever."

His eyes fluttered open, just barely, and he fixed her with a hazy, confused stare. "Why…?" he managed, the word slurring from his lips. "Why are you… helping me?"

Freya crossed her arms, frowning down at him. "Good question. I'm not sure myself." She paused, then added, "Maybe I have a weakness for reckless strangers. Or maybe I'm just a fool."

He let out a faint, breathy chuckle that ended in a cough. "Then... we're even. Both fools."

Freya rolled her eyes, though a faint smile tugged at the corner of her mouth. "Rest while you can. Once you're awake, I expect answers, Firelander."

He closed his eyes again, his expression softening as exhaustion overtook him. She watched him for a moment, studying the lines of his face, the faint remnants of strength that hinted at someone who had seen his own share of trials. Her distrust lingered, but beneath it, curiosity stirred, a reluctant intrigue that she couldn't quite shake.

Turning away, she settled against the wall, her spear resting across her knees as she kept watch over him, her mind racing with questions she didn't dare to ask aloud.

Freya glanced around the small shelter, its icy walls barely shielding them from the biting wind. She'd dragged Tarek as far inside as possible, positioning him against the sturdiest part of the wall where the chill was slightly less biting. The dim light made his face look even paler, his breaths shallow but steady. For a moment, Freya just looked at him, her mind a mess of warring thoughts.

"Firelander…" she muttered, shaking her head as she knelt beside him. "Of all people…"

She reached out, hesitating as her hand hovered over his cloak. The flame insignia glinted faintly, its intricate pattern of black and red twisting like smoke frozen into the fabric. Her fingers pulled back instinctively, her eyes narrowing as she studied it. The emblem was a reminder, as bold as if he'd announced it aloud, that their people were enemies, their lives forged in conflict.

"What are you even doing here?" she murmured, half to herself, half to the unconscious man lying beside her. "Did you think you could just waltz into Icefolk territory without consequence?"

He shifted slightly, murmuring something incomprehensible in his sleep, his brows furrowing as if caught in a dream. Freya's fingers clenched, her instinct to pull away fighting with her sense of duty. She knew she should be on guard, that a Firelander was nothing but trouble in her world, and yet… here she was, practically offering him shelter.

"You'd probably leave me here if our roles were reversed, wouldn't you?" she muttered, the bitterness in her voice barely hiding the uncertainty beneath it.

Freya sighed, glancing around the shelter. She knew he'd be even worse off without some kind of warmth. Pulling her cloak tighter around herself, she unfastened a flask from her belt and poured a small amount of water into her hand, patting it gently across his forehead, hoping the damp coolness would rouse him a little.

"Come on," she whispered, more to herself than to him. "Wake up, Firelander. I don't have all night."

Tarek's eyes fluttered, a low groan escaping his lips as he struggled back to consciousness. Slowly, his gaze fixed on her, his eyes still clouded but holding a spark of awareness. He seemed to focus on her face, confusion mixing with wariness.

"Who… who are you?" His voice was barely a whisper, thick with exhaustion, but the defiance in his tone was unmistakable.

"Someone who's trying to keep you from freezing to death," she replied flatly, raising an eyebrow. "Not that I'm sure why."

Tarek blinked, his gaze shifting down to her hands as she reached into her pack, retrieving a strip of cloth. "And… why should I trust you?"

Freya snorted softly, rolling her eyes. "You don't have much of a choice, do you?" She held up the cloth, her expression unreadable. "This is to wrap your hands. You're close to frostbite."

"Frostbite?" His eyes flickered, a hint of irritation breaking through the fog of his exhaustion. "Never had a problem with it before."

"Well, you're clearly not invincible." She placed the cloth over his hands, working with brisk, efficient movements. "You shouldn't even be here, Firelander. This place is no friend to outsiders, especially not to you."

A faint smirk tugged at his lips, despite the strain in his face. "Didn't... realize the mountain kept a list of favorites."

Freya shot him a look, a mix of frustration and curiosity glinting in her eyes. "Why are you here, then? What could be worth risking your life for in this place?"

Tarek's smirk faded, his gaze turning distant. He didn't answer, simply watching her as she finished wrapping his hands, the silence between them stretching taut.

She huffed, shifting uncomfortably as she leaned back. "You don't have to tell me," she muttered, her voice laced with irritation. "It's not like I care."

"Then why... help me?" he asked, his voice quiet, though there was a sharpness beneath the fatigue.

Freya froze, his question hanging in the air like a challenge. She didn't answer immediately, her mind racing as she tried to come up with an answer that made sense, even to herself. "Because," she began, faltering. "Because it's... it's what a Guardian would do."

"A Guardian?" His brow furrowed, the confusion in his gaze deepening. "You don't look like one of the Guardians I've heard about."

Her jaw tightened, and for a split second, a flicker of anger flashed across her face. "That's because I'm not one anymore," she said, her voice low, almost as if the admission pained her. "Not in the way you'd think."

He studied her, his expression softening slightly as he seemed to sense the weight of her words. "So, what are you now?"

Freya paused, caught off guard by the question. She opened her mouth to answer, but found herself at a loss. She had been stripped of the title, cast out by her people, and yet… here she was, still acting as though she had a duty to uphold.

"I… I don't know," she admitted finally, her voice barely more than a whisper. "Maybe I'm just… lost. Or maybe I'm trying to make up for something I can't undo."

Tarek watched her, his gaze thoughtful. "Then maybe we're not so different," he murmured, his voice a low rasp that seemed to echo her own regret.

She looked away, her fists clenching as she fought back the emotions threatening to surface. She couldn't afford to show weakness, not here, not to him. "Rest," she ordered, her tone hardening as she turned back to him, regaining her composure. "I didn't drag you in here just to listen to your sad story."

He gave her a faint, tired smile, closing his eyes. "Could've fooled me," he murmured, the hint of humor in his voice both infuriating and strangely comforting.

Freya scoffed, leaning back against the wall, her gaze fixed on the shadows outside the shelter. Her thoughts swirled, her mind divided between frustration, curiosity, and a faint, reluctant sense of connection. She still didn't trust him—not fully. But something about his presence, his own struggles, resonated in a way she hadn't expected.

She closed her eyes, letting the silence settle between them, each of them wrapped in their own thoughts, bound by a shared, unspoken understanding that neither would admit aloud.

Tarek's breaths were slow and shallow, but the hint of color returning to his cheeks suggested that he was starting to come around. Freya sat a few paces away, one hand resting on her spear, her gaze sharp and watchful. Shadows flickered across the shelter as the last light of dusk slipped away, and the temperature plummeted, turning every breath into a visible cloud of mist.

She watched him stir, a faint groan escaping his lips as he shifted, the pain flickering across his face like a shadow. Freya's grip on her spear tightened instinctively. She had no idea who he really was, nor why he was here in the Glacial Rift. But a Firelander, this far into Icefolk territory? It wasn't exactly a casual journey. Whatever brought him here, it had to be serious. Or foolish.

"Finally awake, are we?" she muttered, her voice edged with caution as she kept her distance.

Tarek's eyes fluttered open, still clouded with confusion, his gaze moving slowly around the small shelter before settling on her. He blinked, as if trying to piece together where he was, then gave a faint, crooked smile. "So… you didn't just leave me to freeze, then?" His voice was hoarse, and the accent—a soft, rolling cadence with a hint of fire to each word—marked him unmistakably as a Firelander.

Freya raised an eyebrow, her expression impassive. "No, but don't start thinking that means I trust you." She shifted her grip on the spear, making her caution clear. "Saving your life doesn't mean I'll spare it if you give me a reason."

Tarek let out a soft, almost amused breath. "Wouldn't expect anything less from an Icefolk. Suspicion's in your blood, isn't it?"

She narrowed her eyes. "I wouldn't speak so boldly if I were the one lying half-dead in a stranger's shelter. I could have left you for the mountain wolves, you know."

"Yet here I am," he murmured, his gaze thoughtful as he regarded her. "Which begs the question… why?"

Freya hesitated, unable to answer immediately. The truth was, she hadn't been sure herself. Part of her wanted to turn and walk away, to let this stranger's fate remain his own. But something in his appearance—a hint of familiar pain beneath the rugged exterior—had kept her there. She cleared her throat, evading his question.

"What are you doing here, Firelander?" she asked instead, her voice firm, refusing to let him steer the conversation. "This is no place for your kind."

Tarek let out a weak chuckle, his eyes darkening with a mix of defiance and weariness. "No place for anyone, really. But I could say the same about you. What's an Ice Guardian doing so far out here… all alone?"

Freya's jaw tightened. "That's none of your business."

"Touchy, aren't we?" He shifted, wincing as he adjusted his position. His gaze flickered, and for a moment, something unreadable passed across his face. "Maybe we're not so different, you and I."

She scoffed. "Don't flatter yourself."

Tarek's lips curled into a faint smile, though there was a bitterness beneath it. "You don't even know me. You don't know… what I've lost." His voice trailed off, his gaze distant, as if he were looking somewhere far beyond the confines of the shelter.

Freya's eyes narrowed, the faintest hint of curiosity stirring beneath her wariness. "Lost?" she echoed, watching him carefully. "What could you possibly have in common with me?"

He let out a short, humorless laugh. "More than you'd think." His voice softened, barely more than a whisper. "Betrayal… it has a way of shaping a person. Makes you see things differently. Makes you… question everything you once held as truth."

Freya's heart clenched, the word echoing in her mind like a distant bell. Betrayal. It was a word she knew all too well, a wound that had never fully healed, a reminder of why she was here, alone in the mountains. Her grip on the spear loosened, just slightly, as she regarded him with something approaching understanding.

"So," she said carefully, her tone softer but guarded. "You were betrayed?"

Tarek's eyes met hers, a flicker of something dark and haunted behind them. "You could say that," he murmured, his voice rough. "By those I thought would… stand by me. But people… they're fickle. Loyalties are as fragile as ice."

She looked away, his words striking closer than she wanted to admit. "Then why come here? Why the Glacial Rift?"

Tarek hesitated, his gaze lowering, as if weighing whether or not to answer. "I could ask the same of you, couldn't I? This place…" He took a shuddering breath, pausing. "It calls to those who have nowhere else to go."

Freya bit her lip, a quiet anger flaring up within her. "Maybe," she replied, the words clipped, "but I didn't come here to… reminisce over past hurts with a Firelander."

A smirk ghosted over Tarek's face, though it didn't reach his eyes. "Trust me, Guardian… that's not my idea of a good time either."

Freya studied him, the hardness in her gaze softening just a fraction. For the first time since finding him, she felt a sliver of connection—a reluctant recognition that they might share more than she had assumed. She caught herself, frowning, reminding herself of who he was. But she couldn't deny the quiet, unspoken understanding between them, a shared weight of exile, betrayal, and isolation.

"Well, don't get too comfortable," she said finally, the edge returning to her voice. "This isn't some act of charity. Once you're strong enough to walk, we're going our separate ways. I've got my own problems to deal with."

"Believe me," Tarek replied, settling back with a weary sigh, "I'm not looking to make friends." He closed his eyes, though the faintest hint of a smile tugged at his lips. "But maybe fate has other plans."

Freya scoffed, rolling her eyes. "I don't believe in fate."

"Then what do you believe in?" he murmured, his voice soft, the question lingering in the air as he drifted back into uneasy rest.

She didn't answer, the question striking deeper than she wanted to admit. Instead, she tightened her cloak around her shoulders, her gaze fixed on the darkness outside the shelter, her thoughts churning with doubts and memories she had tried so hard to bury.

The shelter was quiet except for the soft crackle of wind outside, echoing through the narrow crevices in the rock. Freya sat across from Tarek, watching him with guarded eyes. His breathing had steadied, the tension in his face softening as he rested, though she could tell his body was still worn and weary. The air between them was thick with unspoken words, both of them too cautious—or perhaps too stubborn—to break the silence.

Freya shifted, adjusting her cloak as she finally spoke. "You're lucky I didn't leave you out there," she muttered, more to herself than to him. "Most of my people wouldn't have hesitated."

Tarek opened one eye, a faint smirk tugging at his lips. "Then I suppose I should thank the stars it was you and not 'most of your people,'" he replied, his voice still rough but tinged with wry humor. "Though I imagine you're not thrilled with the company either."

She gave a small, reluctant shrug. "I'm still not sure why I bothered," she admitted, her tone blunt. "You're a Firelander. That alone should've been enough reason to keep walking."

"Then why didn't you?" he asked, his voice softening, a curious light in his eyes as he met her gaze.

Freya hesitated, glancing down at her hands. She wasn't sure she had an answer, or at least, not one she was willing to share. "I don't know. Maybe I just didn't want your ghost haunting this place," she replied dryly, deflecting with a touch of sarcasm.

"Ah, so it's mercy wrapped in pragmatism," Tarek replied with a smirk. "Good to know."

She rolled her eyes, though a faint smile tugged at the corner of her lips. "Don't get comfortable. As soon as you can stand on your own, we're parting ways. This is temporary, nothing more."

"Agreed," Tarek replied, his expression turning serious. "I'm not here for companionship either." He paused, his gaze slipping past her, as though he could see something beyond the shelter walls. "But… I won't deny, the company is appreciated, if only for the night."

Freya looked at him, sensing a quiet vulnerability in his words. It was strange, hearing it from someone who wore the insignia of her enemies, someone whose people had likely fought against hers more times than she cared to count. And yet, she felt the same sense of isolation clinging to him, a shadow that mirrored her own.

"What brought you here, anyway?" she asked, her tone softer, though still guarded. "The Rift is hardly a place you stumble into by accident."

Tarek hesitated, his fingers brushing the edges of his cloak. "You're right. This was no accident," he admitted, his voice low. "I'm looking for… answers, I suppose. Redemption, maybe." He chuckled softly, but the sound held no humor. "Though I doubt the mountain has much forgiveness to offer."

Freya's expression softened, the hint of shared understanding glinting in her eyes. "It doesn't," she replied, almost a whisper. "But sometimes… it's all that's left."

They fell into silence, the weight of their words hanging between them. Freya shifted, glancing away, as if the intimacy of the conversation unsettled her.

"So," she said, clearing her throat, "are you expecting me to keep watch, or should I assume you can fend for yourself if trouble comes knocking?"

Tarek chuckled, his eyes bright with a hint of mischief. "Don't worry, Guardian. I may be battered, but I'm far from defenseless."

Freya's brow lifted. "I'm not a Guardian," she said, the words coming out sharper than she intended. "Not anymore."

He studied her for a moment, his gaze steady. "You say that like it's the whole truth," he replied, his tone calm, yet somehow knowing. "But you're here, alone, in the Rift, and something tells me that wasn't by choice."

She looked away, jaw tightening. "You don't know anything about me."

"You're right," he replied with a slight nod. "But I know enough about people like us… to recognize the shadows we carry."

Freya opened her mouth to argue, but the words died in her throat. Instead, she let out a quiet sigh, feeling the weight of exhaustion settle over her. She leaned back, pulling her cloak tighter around her shoulders, casting one last glance at Tarek as he settled against the shelter wall.

"This doesn't change anything," she said firmly, as though reminding herself as much as him. "In the morning, we go our separate ways. I won't be responsible for whatever trouble you bring."

"Understood," Tarek replied, his tone soft but unwavering. "I wouldn't expect anything more."

They shared a long, steady look, the silence between them thick but strangely comfortable, an unspoken agreement passing in the brief meeting of their eyes. Freya finally relaxed, allowing herself to settle back against the cold wall, her gaze fixed on the entrance of the shelter, where the snow swirled in a silent storm outside.

As she closed her eyes, sleep slowly creeping in, she found her mind drifting against her will. She thought of the journey that lay ahead, of the challenges she'd face alone, and… of the man beside her, the Firelander with a haunted gaze and a story she couldn't yet unravel.

In the silence of the night, as the darkness deepened, she felt something shift within her—a spark of curiosity she couldn't quite shake, a flicker of doubt she couldn't quite dismiss.

"What are you hiding, Tarek?" she whispered, more to herself than to him.

He stirred slightly, as if hearing her voice even in his sleep, and Freya quickly shut her eyes, pushing the questions aside. She forced herself to drift off, reminding herself that this alliance, this moment of shared silence, was only temporary. Tomorrow, they would part ways, and she'd be alone once more, her path unburdened by the presence of a Firelander stranger.

And yet, as she finally fell into a restless sleep, her mind kept circling back to him, to the mystery he carried, and to the quiet, unspoken understanding that had passed between them—a bond forged in shadows, in silence, and in a night neither of them would soon forget.

Chapter 3
Strangers and Survival

The wind had softened to a low murmur as Freya and Tarek trekked across a narrow ledge, the tension between them still thick from their encounter with the Frost Seraph. The silence weighed on them, a fragile truce barely holding as they each navigated their own guarded thoughts. They had traveled in near silence for what felt like hours, their footsteps echoing against the cold stone cliffs.

Suddenly, a figure emerged from the shadows, slipping from the jagged rock face with a grace that was almost otherworldly. Freya halted, her instincts honed on alert, and Tarek, catching her movement, turned sharply to follow her gaze.

The figure, tall and lean with an ethereal air about him, seemed to blend seamlessly with the darkness, his pale skin catching only fragments of the wan light. He wore a cloak as black as the night itself, edges swirling like shadows around him. His eyes, a piercing shade of silver, regarded them with a faint, unsettling curiosity.

"Who…?" Tarek began, his voice trailing off as the stranger lifted a gloved hand in a silencing gesture.

"Eirwen," the man introduced himself, his voice a soft, whispering tone that slid into the air like a hidden blade. "I've been watching you."

Freya's hand tightened on her spear, her voice guarded. "Watching us?"

"Only to see if you were worth the trouble," Eirwen replied, his gaze shifting from Freya to Tarek, assessing them with a detached, clinical calm. "I had my doubts, but here you are."

Tarek raised an eyebrow, unimpressed. "And you just happened to be lurking around, waiting for the right moment to show yourself?"

A faint smile played on Eirwen's lips, though it held no warmth. "The mountain has eyes, Firelander. I am merely one of them."

Freya studied him, her expression wary. "Why reveal yourself now? We've survived without your help."

"Perhaps," Eirwen murmured, stepping closer, his figure melting in and out of the shadows as though he was part of them. "But the mountain's trials grow harsher as you climb, and not all of them can be faced with fire and ice alone. If you wish to reach the summit, you will need someone who knows its secrets."

"And that would be you, I take it?" Tarek asked, a skeptical note in his voice.

"Indeed." Eirwen's gaze flickered over Tarek, a glint of amusement in his eyes. "Unless, of course, you believe your flames are sufficient to melt every shadow in your path."

Tarek's jaw tightened, but he held his ground. "We don't need your help. We've made it this far on our own."

Freya glanced at Tarek, her eyes narrowed. "And how much farther do you think we'll get if the mountain itself decides to turn on us?"

Eirwen's smile widened, his voice dipping to a low murmur. "Wise words, Ice Guardian. The mountain has its own will, and it is rarely kind to those who tread its paths alone."

"Why should we trust you?" Freya asked, her tone cold, a glint of challenge in her gaze. "You appear out of nowhere, claiming knowledge, but how do we know you're not another trial the mountain has thrown in our way?"

Eirwen's gaze softened, a shadow of something unreadable passing across his features. "Trust, Ice Guardian, is a luxury. I offer guidance, not companionship. Follow, or don't. It makes little difference to me."

Tarek let out a low chuckle, crossing his arms. "Helpful. Really inspires confidence."

"Confidence," Eirwen echoed, his tone almost mocking as he looked at Tarek. "Is often misplaced in those who think themselves invulnerable. But confidence does not keep you alive out here." He turned, as if inviting them to follow, yet his words carried an edge of finality. "It is choice, Firelander. Your choice."

Freya exchanged a quick glance with Tarek, her voice dropping to a low whisper. "He might be the only one who knows what we're truly up against. This isn't a place for pride."

Tarek's expression was skeptical, but he gave a resigned nod. "Fine. But one wrong move, and he finds out how hot fire can burn."

Eirwen's silver gaze shifted to them both, as if hearing the unspoken exchange, and a faint gleam of approval flickered in his eyes. "Wise indeed. Trust may be a luxury, but survival is not."

He stepped back into the shadows, his movements fluid, barely disturbing the air around him. "Follow me, and perhaps we will reach the summit together," he whispered, his voice merging with the mountain wind, a murmur of secrets that only the mountain itself could know.

Freya and Tarek hesitated only a moment longer, then fell into step behind him, their steps careful, their hearts wary, as Eirwen led them deeper into the shadows of the mountain.

As Eirwen led them deeper along the mountain's shadowed path, Freya felt her unease deepen, coiling in her chest like a storm ready to break. Eirwen moved with an unsettling grace, his form blurring with the shadows, barely distinguishable from the cold stone around them. Her instincts, honed from years as an Ice Guardian, screamed at her to tread carefully, not only with the mountain but with this new "guide" who had slipped from the shadows.

Freya's eyes narrowed as she watched Eirwen's movements, observing every subtle flicker of his gaze, every calculated step. She slowed her pace, letting Tarek catch up beside her, and placed a steadying hand on his arm, pulling him aside as Eirwen continued ahead.

"Freya, what—" Tarek began, glancing at her hand on his arm.

"We need to talk," she interrupted, her voice low but firm. She cast a wary glance toward Eirwen, who was now a few paces ahead, his figure barely visible in the growing shadows. "About him."

Tarek followed her gaze, his expression mildly exasperated. "Eirwen? He may be unsettling, but he knows the terrain better than we do. I'd think you'd be the last person to refuse any advantage, Freya."

"It's not that simple," she said, her tone sharp, the weight of her words sinking into the cold air. "I don't trust him."

Tarek arched an eyebrow. "Not that I trust him either, but that seems like the least of our worries. He's the first sign of help we've had since we crossed into the Rift."

Freya's hand tightened on his arm, a flicker of urgency in her eyes. "You don't know him like I do. Eirwen has... a reputation in the Northlands. His loyalties are as thin as frost, and he's known for shifting alliances when it suits him. He doesn't stand by anyone unless there's something in it for himself."

Tarek studied her, frowning. "What do you mean, 'you know him'? This isn't the first time you've crossed paths?"

Freya hesitated, the past bubbling up despite her best efforts to keep it buried. "Eirwen was once a Guardian in training, like I was. But he was… different. Detached. Always lurking in the background, observing rather than engaging. He was more interested in the secrets of the mountain than in serving Heart Village."

"So he's an outcast?" Tarek's tone was cautious, probing.

Freya's gaze hardened, her voice barely above a whisper. "Outcast is putting it kindly. He was cast out for meddling with forbidden practices—things that twisted the nature of his magic. Ice Guardians aren't supposed to deal in shadows. But Eirwen… he embraced it, twisted his abilities into something dark, unnatural. The council couldn't risk keeping him near the village, so they exiled him. No one's seen him since."

Tarek's eyes flicked back to where Eirwen's figure melded with the dimly lit path, his expression guarded. "And yet he's here. Conveniently, right when we need him most."

"Exactly." Freya's tone was grim, laced with suspicion. "His timing is too perfect. People don't just appear in the Rift without a purpose, especially not people like him."

"Then what do you think he wants?" Tarek's gaze returned to hers, a spark of intrigue mixed with wariness.

"That's what worries me." Freya released a slow breath, glancing toward Eirwen's retreating figure. "I've seen the way he looks at this mountain—like it's something he owns, something he's mastered. Whatever he's guiding us toward, it's not for our benefit. Eirwen doesn't help people. He manipulates them."

Tarek took in her words, nodding slowly, his voice quiet but resolved. "So we watch him, closely. Let him lead us, but never lose sight of his intentions."

Freya nodded, a flicker of relief in her eyes. "Agreed. I'd rather have him where I can see him than lurking behind us. But keep your guard up. If he makes any sudden moves, we can't hesitate."

Tarek glanced at Eirwen, who had paused a few steps ahead, his figure still and almost statuesque in the fading light. "You know, I thought your people were supposed to be stoic, patient, almost serene," he murmured, giving her a teasing look. "You, Freya, are decidedly... intense."

A reluctant smile tugged at her lips, though her voice remained serious. "This mountain changes people. I'll take intensity over carelessness any day."

Tarek shrugged, the hint of a grin in his expression. "Fair enough. But don't worry—I'm watching him as closely as you are. If he tries anything, he'll have both fire and ice to answer to."

Freya gave him a nod of approval, her gaze steady. "Good. Remember that, Tarek. Out here, trust is a weapon, and we can't afford to give him ours."

As they resumed their pace, closing the distance to Eirwen, the unspoken understanding between them held firm. They would follow the shadowed path, but with eyes wide open, prepared to meet whatever hidden motives Eirwen carried.

Eirwen moved through the mountain's twisted paths with the ease of someone entirely at home, his steps so light they seemed to leave no trace on the ground. Freya and Tarek followed close behind, navigating narrow ridges and steep climbs, every sense on high alert. Despite her reservations, Freya couldn't deny the unerring accuracy with which Eirwen guided them, avoiding dead ends and hidden chasms as if he'd memorized every inch of the treacherous terrain.

"Here," Eirwen called softly, his voice barely more than a whisper as he gestured toward a narrow path almost concealed by hanging ice. "This way."

Freya hesitated, her gaze sweeping over the seemingly invisible route, then to Eirwen's shadowed figure. "How do you know these paths so well?"

Eirwen's lips curved in a faint smile, his silver eyes gleaming. "I know what the mountain permits me to know."

Tarek raised an eyebrow, glancing at Freya with a faint smirk. "Cryptic. Doesn't that make you feel reassured?"

Freya's gaze remained steady, her suspicion simmering just beneath the surface. "The mountain doesn't just reveal itself to anyone."

Eirwen chuckled softly, his voice slipping through the air like a ghostly wind. "You're right, Freya. But it's more willing to speak to those who listen." He turned back to the path, his movements fluid and measured. "Come along, unless you wish to linger and test your luck with the night's creatures."

Tarek cast Freya a sidelong glance as they started after him. "He's certainly… unique."

"That's one way to put it," Freya muttered, eyes trained on Eirwen's back as he led them forward.

After several quiet steps, Tarek whispered to Freya, "You really don't trust him, do you?"

Freya's expression didn't soften. "I know what he's capable of. I'm not about to turn my back on him."

Tarek's gaze flicked to Eirwen, who was gliding ahead, seeming to dissolve in and out of the shadows as they deepened around him. "But… look at him. He hasn't led us astray. It almost seems like he's gone out of his way to keep us from danger."

"Almost," Freya murmured, her voice taut. "People like him don't help out of kindness."

"So you're saying he's incapable of a decent motive?" Tarek's voice carried a hint of skepticism, though he kept his voice low.

Freya shot him a sharp look. "This isn't about kindness or trust. Eirwen serves his own ends. He'll lead us where he wants to lead us—he just hasn't shown his hand yet."

Ahead of them, Eirwen's voice floated back, eerily aware of the conversation behind him. "You're right, Ice Guardian. I have my own interests, but they don't necessarily work against yours."

Freya's gaze hardened, her tone as cold as the mountain air. "Forgive me if that isn't comforting."

Eirwen chuckled, pausing to glance over his shoulder. "Comfort is for those who have the luxury to need it. You and I, Freya, we're past such luxuries."

Tarek interrupted, his voice skeptical but searching. "Then tell me, Eirwen, what exactly are your 'interests' here?"

Eirwen's expression softened with something that might have been amusement or perhaps a tinge of pity. "Firelander, I am interested in what lies at the heart of this mountain. A power that few understand, but all would wield if they could."

"So it's power you're after?" Freya asked, her tone a mix of accusation and resignation.

Eirwen inclined his head slightly, neither confirming nor denying. "Power, knowledge… call it what you will. But this mountain holds secrets older than either of our lands. And I, unlike you, have spent years learning how to hear them."

Freya's eyes narrowed. "Secrets like the Seraph we encountered?"

Eirwen's lips twitched in the shadow of a smile. "The Seraph was a test—a taste of the mountain's memory, if you will. It has more to offer for those who are willing to seek it."

Tarek studied him, frowning. "And you think we're just going to help you? Blindly walk wherever you lead?"

Eirwen's gaze was unreadable, his voice almost gentle. "Help? No. I don't need your help, Firelander. I am your guide—nothing more, nothing less."

Freya shook her head, a bitter edge to her words. "A guide only takes you where they want you to go."

Eirwen tilted his head, his voice softening, taking on a peculiar note of melancholy. "Then perhaps, Freya, you should decide where you want to go. I simply offer the path. The choice, as always, is yours."

Freya and Tarek exchanged a glance, both unsettled by his words yet strangely drawn forward by the conviction in his tone. There was something in the way he spoke of the mountain, as if he were not merely its servant, but its instrument, bound to its secrets in ways they couldn't fathom.

Tarek sighed, keeping his voice low as they followed Eirwen's shadowy figure. "You may not trust him, Freya, but maybe… maybe he's just what we need right now."

Freya's response was barely a whisper, her gaze fixed on the path ahead. "We'll see. But don't forget, Tarek… shadows are deceptive."

Eirwen led them onward, his form merging seamlessly with the darkness, and as they moved, Freya could feel the weight of the mountain's presence pressing in, watching, listening. She gritted her teeth, resolved to stay vigilant.

The path narrowed as they continued to climb, jagged rock walls pressing in around them, casting deep shadows that stretched and distorted with every step. Eirwen moved ahead, his dark form almost blending into the mountain, his gait steady and unfazed. Behind him, Tarek and Freya exchanged wary glances, each trying to decipher the mystery of their guide and his unsettling words.

The silence felt heavy until Eirwen stopped abruptly, his gaze fixed on the horizon where a faint glow of twilight painted the sky. He stood there, quiet and still, and it was only after a moment that he spoke, his voice low, reverberating with something like reverence.

"There's a storm coming," he murmured, more to himself than to them.

Tarek furrowed his brow, looking up at the clear expanse. "A storm? The sky's barely even cloudy."

Eirwen turned, a ghostly smile tugging at the corners of his mouth. "Not every storm reveals itself in clouds and rain, Firelander. Some storms are felt rather than seen. They stir the spirit, test its mettle." He paused, his silver gaze darkening. "And this mountain… it doesn't forgive the unprepared."

Freya's eyes narrowed, suspicion flickering in her gaze. "You speak as if the mountain has its own will."

Eirwen nodded slowly, his tone holding an eerie calm. "It does. The mountain is alive in ways you wouldn't understand, Ice Guardian. It holds memories, grudges, even desires. And it rewards or punishes as it sees fit."

Tarek let out a quiet chuckle, though his amusement was tinged with doubt. "You make it sound like we're dealing with some ancient spirit."

Eirwen's gaze settled on him, intense and unwavering. "Perhaps you are."

Freya's jaw tightened, her tone cool. "If there's something we need to know, Eirwen, I suggest you stop speaking in riddles and tell us directly."

Eirwen tilted his head, considering her words. "Very well. The path we follow grows more dangerous with each step. There are forces in this mountain that despise outsiders, that resent the fire in your veins, Tarek, and the frost in yours, Freya."

Freya raised an eyebrow, unimpressed. "That's hardly news. Everything in this place has tried to kill us since we arrived."

Eirwen's expression didn't change, his voice unyielding. "What you've faced so far is nothing compared to what lies ahead. You've been treading the edge, but soon, you will enter the heart of the mountain. And it has defenses that go beyond mere creatures or specters."

Tarek glanced at Freya, intrigued despite himself. "And what exactly are these defenses? More Frost Seraphs?"

Eirwen's voice dropped to a murmur, as if sharing a dark secret. "The mountain's heart is guarded by shades older than memory, protectors bound by an oath to ensure no living soul reaches the summit without permission. They sense fear, doubt… even intent. And they show mercy to no one."

Freya's eyes hardened, her voice edged with defiance. "If that's supposed to scare us, it won't work. We came here prepared for whatever challenge this mountain has."

A faint smirk flickered across Eirwen's lips, but his gaze held a strange, shadowed sorrow. "I don't offer warnings to frighten you, Freya. I only tell you the truth. The mountain doesn't care for intentions. It recognizes only strength… and resilience."

Tarek let out a slow breath, his expression caught between skepticism and intrigue. "You talk about this place like it's sacred, almost as if it's alive."

Eirwen inclined his head, a faint shimmer of approval in his eyes. "You're beginning to understand, Firelander. This mountain was here before either of our lands knew fire or frost. It remembers what we've forgotten."

Freya's patience was wearing thin, her suspicion intensifying. "And what is your role in all this, Eirwen? Why are you here? You speak of the mountain's will, but you're no guardian. You're an outcast."

Eirwen's eyes glinted with something unreadable, a flicker of emotion buried beneath his calm demeanor. "Outcast, yes. But that does not mean I lack purpose. The mountain and I… have an understanding. I am here as its guide, its voice when it chooses silence."

"So you're telling us," Tarek began slowly, trying to make sense of Eirwen's cryptic words, "that this mountain has granted you… permission to be here?"

"Permission," Eirwen echoed with a soft, almost mocking smile. "Or tolerance, if you prefer. The mountain does not see me as a threat. I move as it allows, as I have learned to listen."

Freya crossed her arms, a doubtful edge in her tone. "And what happens if it changes its mind? What happens if it no longer 'tolerates' you?"

Eirwen's gaze met hers, steady and unblinking. "Then I will be the first to know. And so will you." He let the words hang in the air, his voice soft but chilling, the unspoken threat woven through each syllable.

Freya clenched her fists, an unyielding spark in her eyes. "I don't care how much you revere this mountain or what deals you've struck with it, Eirwen. We came here for our own reasons, and I won't be swayed by your stories of shadows and ancient oaths."

Eirwen's gaze lingered on her, a hint of something almost like admiration in his expression. "Strength of will, Ice Guardian. But remember… willpower alone doesn't guarantee survival here. Respect the mountain, or it will remind you why you should."

Tarek watched the exchange, his own suspicion tempered by curiosity. He glanced at Freya, his voice quiet but contemplative. "Maybe he's right, Freya. We've already seen things here we can't explain. If there's truth in his warnings…"

Freya's gaze hardened, though a faint flicker of doubt crossed her face. "If he's right, we'll handle it when the time comes. But until then, we move on our own terms."

Eirwen gave a slight nod, his expression unreadable. "Very well. But remember my words, both of you. This mountain is no mere obstacle. It is an entity unto itself. And it has watched over more lives than you could ever count."

With that, he turned, his figure dissolving into the shadows ahead, leaving Freya and Tarek standing in the dim, uncertain light. Tarek watched him go, a glint of intrigue still in his eyes.

"Freya," he said, his voice soft but insistent, "you may not trust him, but there's something about him… something more than meets the eye."

Freya sighed, her gaze locked on the path ahead, where Eirwen's shadowy form had disappeared. "I'll keep my eye on him, Tarek. But I won't let his riddles lead us astray." She tightened her grip on her spear, determination hardening in her stance. "Let's go. We're not losing sight of him."

They pressed on, shadows pooling around them as they followed Eirwen's trail, a quiet resolve strengthening in each step, though questions lingered unanswered in the silence.

Chapter 4
A Mysterious Guide

The wind howled through the narrow pass, carrying with it a biting cold that clung to Freya and Tarek as they trudged through the snow. Their breaths came in visible clouds, mingling with the mist that clung to the ground in an eerie, otherworldly haze. Freya's eyes were fixed ahead, her body tense, alert to every shadow. But the silence was deceptive, and the snow softened each footfall into ghostly whispers.

"Feels like we're being watched," Tarek murmured, glancing around, his voice barely audible over the wind.

Freya didn't respond immediately, but her hand tightened around the spear she held, her gaze flickering across the cliffs that loomed above them. "It's the mountain," she replied finally, her voice low. "Sometimes it… it has a way of feeling like it's alive."

Tarek snorted, though his gaze remained uneasy. "More than just the mountain, if you ask me. There's something… off."

The mist shifted suddenly, twisting and curling as if caught in an invisible current. Freya's eyes narrowed, her senses prickling as she stopped in her tracks. "Wait," she said sharply, holding up a hand. "Do you feel that?"

Tarek frowned. "Feel what?"

Before Freya could answer, a figure seemed to materialize out of the mist, his form blending seamlessly with the shadows. He moved with a grace that was almost otherworldly, each step soundless as he approached. Freya's breath caught, her instincts screaming a warning. There was something both familiar and unsettling about him, a presence that felt like both a memory and a threat.

"Well, well," the stranger said, his voice smooth, almost amused. "Freya… I see you haven't lost your wariness. That's good. You'll need it."

Freya's grip tightened on her spear, her eyes narrowing. "Who are you? And how do you know my name?"

The man—cloaked in dark furs that seemed to blend into the very mist—smiled faintly, his gaze settling on her with a strange familiarity. "It's been a long time, Freya. I didn't expect to see you here, of all places."

Freya took a step back, her voice guarded. "You didn't answer my question."

"Names… are only useful if they mean something to the other person," he replied smoothly. "But if it gives you peace of mind, you may call me Eirwen."

Tarek shifted beside her, his gaze wary as he sized up the newcomer. "Friend of yours?" he asked, his voice laced with suspicion.

Freya didn't look away from Eirwen, her instincts still on high alert. "No," she said slowly, her voice cold. "At least… not that I know of."

Eirwen's smile deepened, a hint of something enigmatic flickering in his eyes. "We've crossed paths, you and I. Though you may not remember." His gaze lingered on her, a strange intensity in his expression. "But I remember you, Freya. I remember you well."

Freya's jaw tightened, the familiarity in his tone sending a chill down her spine. "What do you want?"

"I might ask you the same," Eirwen replied, tilting his head slightly. "After all, the Glacial Rift isn't exactly a place for… casual wanderers."

"We're here for our own reasons," Freya replied firmly. "And I doubt you're here to offer a warm welcome."

Eirwen chuckled, the sound low and unsettling. "No, I suppose not. But I am here to… guide, let's say. The Rift is unforgiving, and those who enter it unprepared rarely find their way out." His gaze shifted to Tarek, lingering just long enough to make him bristle. "Especially those who don't… belong."

Tarek scoffed, crossing his arms. "And you do? You're not exactly dressed like the rest of her people."

Eirwen's eyes sparkled with amusement. "Perhaps. But the Rift and I have an understanding." He turned back to Freya, his tone softening, almost as if speaking to an old friend. "Freya, you and I share a… connection to this place. The mountain has many secrets, and it remembers those who've walked its paths before."

Freya's eyes narrowed. "What are you talking about?"

Eirwen's gaze was piercing, his voice almost a whisper. "Do you remember nothing? The mountain was once our ally. You walked these paths with me, in a time when you knew the secrets it held."

Freya took a step back, her mind reeling. "That's impossible," she said, her voice tinged with both confusion and denial. "I've never seen you before. I don't know you."

He watched her carefully, his expression unreadable. "Perhaps your memories have faded. Or perhaps… there are things you chose to forget."

"Enough with the riddles," Tarek snapped, his hand resting on the hilt of his blade. "If you have something to say, say it plainly. We're not interested in ghost stories."

Eirwen's gaze flicked to Tarek, his smile faint. "Ah, but the Rift is full of ghosts, Firelander. And if you stay here long enough, you might just become one of them."

Tarek's expression darkened, but Freya held up a hand, stopping him before he could respond. "What are you offering, Eirwen?" she asked, her voice steady but wary. "If you're here to guide us, then what's the price?"

Eirwen's smile softened, though his eyes remained sharp. "I ask for nothing, Freya. Only that you remember. There are trials ahead, tests that will push you to the edge of what you know.

But if you are willing, I can show you the paths through the mountain that others do not see."

Freya hesitated, torn between her instinct to distrust him and the strange pull of familiarity she couldn't explain. "Why should I trust you?" she asked quietly, her voice laced with doubt.

He looked at her for a long moment, his gaze steady. "Because, Freya, deep down… you already do. You may not remember, but trust lingers, even in forgotten memories."

She swallowed, feeling a mixture of unease and reluctant curiosity. "And if I choose to follow?"

Eirwen's gaze softened, almost gentle. "Then you may find the answers you seek. About this mountain. About yourself."

Freya glanced at Tarek, who shook his head, his eyes filled with suspicion. "I don't like this, Freya. We don't even know who he is."

Eirwen's gaze didn't waver, his voice barely more than a whisper. "Sometimes, the path forward isn't about knowing… but remembering."

Freya's heart pounded, her mind swirling with questions. She felt the pull of his words, the strange familiarity of his presence, as if he held a part of her story she had yet to understand.

"All right," she said finally, her voice steady. "Show us the path, Eirwen. But know this—I don't trust you. Not yet."

Eirwen inclined his head, a faint smile on his lips. "Trust is a journey, Freya. One we shall take together."

The snow crunched beneath their feet as they moved through the narrow, winding path Eirwen led them down. The mountain loomed tall and unforgiving around them, and the silence settled heavily, broken only by the occasional gust of wind. Freya's gaze flicked between Eirwen's steady figure ahead and Tarek, who followed close beside her, his posture rigid with suspicion.

"So," Tarek muttered under his breath, his voice laced with sarcasm, "are we just supposed to follow this stranger blindly into the depths of the mountain? Because I don't know about you, Freya, but I'd rather not be led into an ambush."

Freya shot him a sidelong glance. "Believe me, I'm not exactly thrilled about this either," she replied, her voice low but firm. "But he knows this place better than we do. If he can get us through the worst of it…"

Tarek scoffed, crossing his arms. "And what makes you so sure he's not just leading us to our deaths? He seems all too comfortable here for someone wandering this mountain alone."

Eirwen's voice cut through their hushed conversation, smooth and unsettlingly calm. "I can hear you, you know. I assure you, I have no interest in harming either of you. If I did, I wouldn't need to lure you into some 'ambush,' as you so eloquently put it."

Tarek narrowed his eyes, unamused. "Forgive me if I don't take your word for it. You appear out of nowhere, act like you know Freya—"

Eirwen turned his head slightly, his gaze steady. "Because I do know Freya. In ways you couldn't possibly understand."

Freya tensed, caught between the pull of Eirwen's words and the grounding effect of Tarek's skepticism. "Enough of the cryptic comments, Eirwen. If you're going to guide us, at least explain why you're here. Why are you so invested in helping us?"

Eirwen paused, turning fully to face them, his expression calm, almost serene. "Because this mountain holds truths you are both meant to find. Truths that do not reveal themselves to just anyone." His eyes settled on Freya. "And because I have a history with this place… and with you."

Freya's jaw tightened. "What history? I don't know you. You keep saying I should remember, but I don't."

Eirwen's gaze softened, as if he were looking at her through layers of memory. "Not all memories are meant to be remembered at once, Freya. Some… linger, waiting for the right moment to emerge."

Tarek let out a derisive laugh, crossing his arms. "And you're supposed to be the one to 'help' her remember? That sounds convenient. Or maybe it's just your excuse to keep us wandering in circles."

Eirwen smiled faintly, undeterred by Tarek's suspicion. "You're welcome to turn back if you like, Firelander. But I don't imagine you'd fare well alone out here."

Tarek bristled, his hands flexing at his sides. "Oh, I can handle myself, thank you very much. But forgive me if I'm not in the habit of following ghosts who speak in riddles."

Freya stepped between them, sensing the rising tension. "Enough," she said firmly. She looked at Eirwen, her eyes narrowing. "You say you know this place. Fine. But I need more than vague promises. What exactly are we going to face up ahead?"

Eirwen held her gaze, his expression growing serious. "This mountain is… alive, in a way you may not understand. It recognizes those who enter its depths, weighing their intentions, their fears. What you'll face here will not be the typical dangers of ice and snow."

Tarek rolled his eyes, muttering, "Of course, it's 'alive.' More mystic nonsense."

Ignoring him, Eirwen continued, his gaze still fixed on Freya. "The mountain has a way of reflecting what lies within you. Fears, doubts, regrets. If you're not prepared to face them, they'll consume you."

Freya's expression softened, though her voice remained cautious. "And you've... faced these trials?"

Eirwen's eyes darkened, a flicker of something unreadable crossing his face. "I have. And I've emerged with a greater understanding. That's why I'm here. To offer you the guidance I didn't have."

Tarek let out a humorless laugh. "So, what are you? Some sort of... mystical guide who just happens to show up for lost travelers in need of enlightenment?"

Eirwen's gaze shifted to him, calm yet piercing. "Call it what you will, Firelander. But if you're wise, you'll listen rather than mock. The path ahead isn't one you can navigate through brute strength or bravado alone."

Freya glanced between them, caught between Eirwen's steady confidence and Tarek's intense suspicion. She spoke softly, trying to find a balance. "I don't trust you yet, Eirwen. But I've seen enough of this mountain to know it isn't... ordinary."

Eirwen inclined his head, a faint smile tugging at his lips. "Trust isn't necessary, Freya. Only willingness. This path isn't easy, but if you walk it with an open mind, it may reveal things to you... things you need to see."

Tarek shook his head, frustration plain on his face. "And if it's all just an illusion? If this is just a way to trap us here?"

Eirwen's gaze didn't waver. "Then turn back. Leave. But know that the answers you seek will remain here, waiting, whether you're ready for them or not."

Freya felt a strange tug, a pull that seemed to come not from Eirwen, but from the mountain itself, as though something within its depths called to her. She took a deep breath, steadying herself before she turned to Tarek. "I don't like it either," she admitted. "But something… something tells me he might know things we don't. About this place. About why we're here."

Tarek scowled, his gaze fixed on Eirwen. "If he's wrong, if he leads us into danger—"

"Then we'll face it," Freya replied, her voice firmer than she felt. "But we'll face it together."

She looked back at Eirwen, her jaw set, her eyes hard. "If you lead us astray, if this is some kind of trick—"

Eirwen inclined his head, his gaze solemn. "I understand. But I have no intention of betraying you, Freya. My purpose here is not one of harm… but of revelation."

She held his gaze for a moment longer, searching for any hint of deception. Then, reluctantly, she nodded. "Lead the way. But know that we're watching you."

Eirwen smiled faintly, a knowing glint in his eyes. "Good. A little vigilance will serve you well."

As they moved forward, the mountain seemed to grow colder, the shadows deeper, and Freya couldn't shake the feeling that something ancient and watchful lurked just beyond their sight, listening, waiting.

The narrow path wound through the mountain, flanked by sheer drops on one side and jagged cliffs on the other. Freya walked cautiously, her eyes darting from Eirwen's steady pace ahead to the rugged terrain around them. The silence between them had settled thickly, an unspoken tension hanging over their unlikely trio. Eirwen moved with an ease that suggested he knew these paths intimately, while Tarek followed, his jaw clenched and his gaze hard, his distrust toward their mysterious guide palpable.

Eirwen paused, glancing back at them with an enigmatic expression. "You both look tense. Is the path too much for you already?"

Tarek scowled, gripping his cloak tightly. "We're fine," he replied sharply. "Though I'm starting to wonder why you're leading us on this particular path. There's hardly room to breathe."

Eirwen's lips quirked in a faint smile. "Ah, but that's precisely why I chose it. The mountain has many faces, and this one, narrow as it is, is the safest for now. The other paths…" He trailed off, his gaze drifting to the shadowed slopes below. "Let's just say they aren't so kind to travelers."

Freya stepped forward, her voice cold and cautious. "And we're supposed to take your word for it?"

Eirwen's gaze met hers, his eyes steady and unreadable. "Trust, Freya, is earned, not demanded. But I've walked these trails longer than either of you have been alive. If you want to reach the heart of this mountain… you'll need a guide."

Freya bristled, crossing her arms. "And why are you so willing to help us?"

Eirwen tilted his head, his expression thoughtful. "The mountain holds many secrets, ones that aren't revealed to just anyone. But you, Freya… you're not just anyone, are you?"

She tensed, uneasy under his scrutiny. "What's that supposed to mean?"

"It means," he replied, his voice soft and almost reverent, "that you have a history here, whether you remember it or not. And the mountain… it remembers, too."

Freya glanced away, his words unsettling her in ways she couldn't quite explain. She felt Tarek's eyes on her, his expression a mix of skepticism and irritation.

"We don't have time for riddles," Tarek interjected, his tone hard. "Either you're here to help, or you're not. Which is it, Eirwen?"

Eirwen's calm demeanor didn't falter. "Consider my offer this: I can guide you through the most treacherous paths. The mountain will throw obstacles your way—fears, doubts, even the phantoms of your own past. If you want to make it through unscathed, you'll need someone who understands these trials."

Freya's eyes narrowed. "And you're that someone? Just by chance?"

Eirwen chuckled, the sound low and faintly unsettling. "I don't believe in chance, Freya. I believe in purpose. You're here for a reason. And so am I."

Tarek muttered under his breath, his arms crossed tightly. "This sounds like exactly the sort of 'guidance' that could end with us at the bottom of a ravine. Why should we take the risk?"

Eirwen turned his gaze to Tarek, his expression suddenly sharp. "You have questions, Firelander. You want answers. They lie beyond this path, in places you wouldn't survive alone. Do you want them, or not?"

Tarek hesitated, his mouth set in a firm line. His shoulders relaxed slightly, but he didn't look entirely convinced. "Fine. But one misstep, and I'll—"

"You'll do nothing," Eirwen interrupted smoothly, his voice quiet but firm. "Because if I wanted to lead you astray, you'd never know until it was too late."

Freya's hand moved instinctively to her side, fingers brushing the hilt of her dagger. "Is that supposed to comfort us?"

Eirwen's eyes softened, and his voice turned almost gentle. "No, Freya. It's supposed to be honest." He paused, watching her carefully. "If you want to reach the heart of the Rift, you'll need to face things you aren't prepared for. The journey will demand everything from you. But… if you accept my guidance, I can give you a fighting chance."

Freya glanced at Tarek, noting the conflicted look on his face, the tension in his posture. She swallowed, her voice low. "I don't trust you, Eirwen. But… if what you say is true, then I don't have much choice, do I?"

Eirwen inclined his head, his gaze unwavering. "Trust doesn't need to come immediately. But understand this—I'm here to see you through to the other side. The mountain may be merciless, but it can also be a teacher."

Freya's brow furrowed, uncertainty gnawing at her. She looked back at Tarek, catching the doubt flickering in his eyes. "What do you think?" she asked quietly.

Tarek exhaled, his voice begrudging. "I don't like it. But… if he really can get us through this…" He met Eirwen's gaze with steely resolve. "Then I say we take the risk. But don't expect us to lower our guard."

Eirwen offered a small, knowing smile. "Good. A guarded heart is a wise heart in these mountains." He turned, gesturing ahead. "Then follow closely. I'll show you the paths where the mountain shows mercy."

Freya took a steadying breath, forcing herself to take that first step forward, each movement careful, her eyes never leaving Eirwen's back. She kept her voice low, murmuring to Tarek. "Stay close. And don't trust him… no matter what he promises."

"Trust me," Tarek muttered back, his tone dry. "I'm already counting the ways this could go wrong."

Freya gave a faint nod, her grip tightening on her spear. She didn't trust Eirwen. His presence was too convenient, his knowledge too intimate. But the mountain loomed before her, its shadows deep and impenetrable, and she knew that without him, their chances of survival were slim.

"Lead on, Eirwen," she called, her voice steady. "But remember—we're watching you."

Eirwen glanced over his shoulder, his eyes gleaming with a strange light. "Of course, Freya. But remember… sometimes the answers you seek are hidden in the shadows you fear."

And with that, he turned, his form merging once more with the mists that cloaked the path ahead, leaving Freya and Tarek to follow, wary and unwilling, into the heart of the mountain.

The narrow path descended steeply, plunging into shadows where the light barely reached, casting everything in an eerie twilight. Freya adjusted her grip on her spear, her eyes narrowing as she watched Eirwen's form glide ahead of them, barely making a sound as he led them deeper into the mountain's grasp. She exchanged a glance with Tarek, who gave her a slight nod, his hand resting on the hilt of his sword, his every step cautious.

Eirwen paused briefly, looking back over his shoulder. His voice was soft, almost reverent. "The mountain has a will of its own. It doesn't show its paths to just anyone."

Freya frowned, keeping her tone skeptical. "And what makes us so special?"

Eirwen's gaze lingered on her, a flicker of something unreadable in his eyes. "You're here because you have unfinished business… wounds that call to this place. The mountain recognizes such things. It… remembers."

Tarek scoffed, clearly unimpressed. "More riddles. You keep talking as if this place is alive."

Eirwen smiled faintly, continuing to lead them deeper. "The mountain is alive, in its own way. It listens, it watches, and sometimes, if it wills it, it… judges."

Freya shivered, her voice laced with doubt. "And who exactly does it judge, Eirwen? Are we being tested for something, or is this just your way of scaring us?"

He met her gaze, his expression serious. "It judges those who come seeking answers… or absolution. Whatever you seek, it will show you—but only if you're willing to confront what you fear most."

Freya felt her stomach twist, the weight of his words settling over her like a chill. She knew what he was hinting at, could feel the truth in his voice. And yet, she couldn't fully trust him, couldn't ignore the sense that he was leading them somewhere dangerous, somewhere they might not escape.

"So," Tarek said, breaking the tension with a skeptical tone, "if this mountain is so… sentient, why doesn't it just open up and show us the way?"

Eirwen's expression softened, almost as if he found Tarek's question amusing. "Because the mountain reveals itself only to those it deems worthy. It doesn't bend to mere curiosity or arrogance."

Tarek rolled his eyes, muttering under his breath. "Of course. It's all about 'worthiness.' Convenient."

Freya glanced at him, her voice barely more than a whisper. "Maybe it's not so simple, Tarek. There's something… different about this place."

Eirwen's voice cut through their conversation, gentle but firm. "The mountain's purpose is neither convenience nor simplicity. It offers insight to those willing to look deeply, even if the truth isn't easy to accept."

Freya crossed her arms, her expression skeptical. "And you're saying this mountain trusts you?"

Eirwen's eyes held hers steadily. "Trust is a bond earned through trials. It knows me because I've endured its challenges… as you will, in time."

She swallowed, feeling an uncomfortable mix of apprehension and curiosity. She didn't want to admit that something in his words resonated with her, as if he held knowledge she needed, even though she loathed the idea of relying on him.

"What exactly are we supposed to see?" she asked, unable to keep the doubt from her voice.

Eirwen's gaze shifted to the shadows around them, his tone contemplative. "It's different for each person. The mountain shows us reflections of ourselves, fragments of our past, our fears, and the parts of us we'd rather forget."

Freya's heart skipped, his words hitting closer than she wanted. "So, we're just supposed to trust this… this sentient mountain to help us 'find ourselves'? And you, to lead us through it?"

Eirwen's gaze softened. "Trust me, Freya, or don't. But the truth you're seeking lies here. And if you're not willing to confront what the mountain reveals, then you'll never find the answers you came for."

Tarek scoffed, shaking his head. "If this is all one grand scheme to get us lost in some mystical nonsense—"

"It isn't," Eirwen interrupted calmly, his tone unyielding. "Believe what you want, Firelander, but know this: the mountain's tests are unavoidable. You've already set them in motion by stepping onto its paths. The only way forward is through."

Freya exchanged a wary glance with Tarek, uncertainty flickering in her eyes. "You say this like you know what's waiting for us," she said, her tone probing.

Eirwen's expression didn't waver. "I've walked this path before. I've faced my own reflections, my own fears. I emerged… changed. As will you."

Tarek laughed, though the sound was tinged with bitterness. "Changed how? Dead?"

"Possibly," Eirwen replied, his voice soft but unwavering. "But death is not the worst fate for those who lose themselves in these mountains. If you survive, you will be forced to face the truths you've buried."

Freya's hand clenched at her side, her voice low and edged with skepticism. "And you think that's supposed to reassure us?"

Eirwen's gaze held a quiet intensity, a strange empathy she hadn't expected. "Reassurance is a luxury, Freya. I can't promise you comfort, only clarity. And sometimes… clarity is all we have."

Freya took a shaky breath, her mind a storm of conflicting thoughts. Part of her wanted to turn back, to escape the ominous sense of inevitability Eirwen spoke of. But another part of her, the part she couldn't ignore, felt drawn to the idea of facing whatever lay ahead, no matter how dark.

Tarek's voice broke her thoughts. "So, what now? We just keep following you, waiting for this 'truth' to appear?"

Eirwen nodded, his expression serene. "Yes. The mountain will reveal itself in time. Patience, Firelander. The answers don't come to those who rush."

Freya forced herself to nod, though her heart remained heavy with doubt. "Fine. But if you lead us astray…"

Eirwen's eyes softened, a faint sadness in his expression. "If I lead you astray, then I've failed my own path. But trust, Freya… it won't come to that."

With that, he turned, guiding them deeper into the shadows, where the light dwindled and the silence grew heavier. Freya followed, her gaze fixed warily on his back, each step filled with a cautious resolve, torn between mistrust and the inexplicable pull of something she felt she was meant to find.

Chapter 5
Whispers in the Shadows

The path twisted sharply, leading Freya and Tarek to a desolate stretch of rocky ground marked by a jagged, gaping chasm. Heat radiated from the crevice, simmering like a buried inferno, the air thick with the acrid scent of ash and scorched stone. Freya stopped, sensing a shift—a subtle, almost imperceptible tightening in the air. She glanced at Tarek, catching the flicker of uncertainty that crossed his face as he stared into the depths of the chasm.

"Tarek?" she said, her voice cautious.

He didn't answer, his eyes fixed on the dark void before him. Slowly, he took a step closer to the edge, his posture tense, as if drawn toward it by an unseen force. The heat intensified, and with it came the low, taunting echo of a voice he knew all too well.

"Pathetic," it sneered, smooth yet cutting, weaving through the rising flames. "All that fire, all that power—and still, you failed."

Tarek's fists clenched, a muscle in his jaw tightening. He took a sharp breath, trying to shake off the voice, but it persisted, each word a searing reminder of his past. The flames leaped higher, licking at his feet, surrounding him in a blazing, suffocating circle. He felt trapped, as though the mountain itself were bending reality, reshaping it to mirror his own fears.

Freya's voice cut through the rising flames, distant but clear. "Tarek, what's happening?"

He didn't respond, barely hearing her over the growing cacophony of his own doubts. The chasm before him shimmered, revealing a vision within the flames—a familiar figure, tall and imposing, draped in armor that gleamed like polished obsidian. His father. The king he had failed, the one whose approval he had sought his entire life but never gained. The figure's gaze was sharp and penetrating, filled with the contempt that had haunted Tarek since he was old enough to remember.

"Look at you," the apparition said, its voice dripping with disdain. "A disgrace to our bloodline. You think you're worthy of power? You are nothing, Tarek. Nothing but wasted potential."

"Don't... don't say that," Tarek muttered, his voice hoarse, barely audible. But his father's shadowed figure stepped closer, its presence bearing down on him like a storm.

"Are you going to deny it?" The figure sneered, flames flickering in his eyes. "You were given everything—wealth, training, a legacy to uphold—and yet you ran. You chose cowardice. You betrayed your own blood."

Tarek's fists trembled as he tried to steady his breathing, but the anger within him ignited, feeding the flames that danced around his feet, growing higher with each passing moment. "I didn't betray anyone," he whispered, his voice edged with defiance.

The apparition laughed, a harsh, hollow sound that echoed through the chasm. "Then why are you here? Why did you abandon your kingdom, your duty? Running from your failures doesn't absolve them."

Freya's concerned voice broke through his thoughts again, sharper now, edged with worry. "Tarek, talk to me! What are you seeing?"

He forced himself to answer, his voice strained, his gaze never leaving the vision before him. "It's… it's him. My father. The king. He… he thinks I'm a failure." His voice shook, the words spilling out before he could stop them. "He's telling me I was never worthy of the power I was given, that I've done nothing but disgrace my bloodline."

Freya's expression softened, and though she couldn't see the vision he faced, she recognized the pain in his eyes. "Tarek, this is the mountain's trial. It's not real—whatever you're seeing, whatever he's saying, it's meant to provoke you."

Tarek's gaze hardened, his fists clenching tighter. "Real or not, he's right. I did run. I was given everything, and I threw it away because… because I couldn't be the person he wanted me to be."

The flames rose higher, as if feeding off his anger, his doubt, each flickering ember reflecting the accusations that still haunted him. The apparition stepped closer, its face now only inches from his, those familiar, piercing eyes filled with contempt. "You will never be anything but a disgrace, Tarek. You can't control your fire, your anger—because you are weak."

Tarek's jaw tightened, a fire sparking in his own eyes as he met the gaze of his father's ghostly image. "Maybe... maybe I am weak," he said, his voice low, steady. "But I'm done letting your judgment define me. I don't need your approval. Not anymore."

The apparition faltered, the flames around it wavering. Tarek took a step forward, his voice growing stronger, filled with a determination that surprised even him. "You think I'm nothing? Fine. But I'd rather be nothing and find my own path than live by your standards. You can't haunt me anymore. I release you, and I release myself."

With those words, the apparition let out a strangled sound, the flames shuddering before collapsing in on themselves, dissolving into ash that scattered into the air. Tarek stood alone, his breathing steady as he watched the remnants of his past dissipate into the chasm below.

Freya approached, her gaze cautious but sympathetic. "Are you...?"

He nodded, his eyes still fixed on the last flickers of flame. "Yeah. I think... I think I'm okay." He let out a breath he hadn't realized he'd been holding, a weight lifting from his shoulders. "It was just an illusion, but… it felt real. I needed to face it."

Freya placed a hand on his shoulder, her touch grounding. "Sometimes the shadows within us feel the most real. But you did well, Tarek. You faced it. You didn't let it define you."

He met her gaze, a faint smile forming. "Thanks, Freya."

Together, they turned from the edge of the chasm, Tarek's mind clearer, his heart lighter. Whatever lay ahead, he knew he'd taken the first step in freeing himself from the shadows of his past, ready to face whatever trials the mountain had left.

The fiery remnants of Tarek's trial lingered in the air, a haze of ash and embers that crackled around them like the fading echoes of a battle. But as he stepped back from the chasm, a residual heat lingered within him, simmering just beneath the surface. Freya noticed the tension in his stance, the way his fists were clenched so tightly that his knuckles had turned white. His face was taut, eyes dark and unfocused, as if the apparition's accusations still echoed within him, refusing to let go.

"Tarek?" Freya's voice was calm, her tone gentle but edged with concern.

He didn't respond, his breathing growing more ragged as the flames flickered to life around his hands, small sparks at first, but they quickly grew, licking up his arms, fueled by the anger and frustration that he'd tried so hard to suppress. His jaw tightened, and he looked at his own hands with a mix of horror and helplessness, unable to control the fire that was spiraling out of him.

"Tarek," Freya said, more firmly this time, stepping closer. "Look at me. You need to calm down."

His gaze snapped to hers, but his eyes were wild, flames reflecting in their depths. "Calm down?" he bit out, his voice filled with raw emotion. "Do you have any idea what it feels like? To live with that… that constant shadow of expectation, of knowing that I'll never measure up, no matter what I do?"

Freya didn't flinch, keeping her eyes steady on him. "I know what it feels like to carry a weight that seems impossible to bear. But this—" She gestured to the flames rising around him, her tone unwavering. "This isn't helping you. Let it go, Tarek."

He shook his head, his voice trembling with suppressed rage. "Let it go? How am I supposed to let it go when every step I take, I feel that judgment, that scorn? Even in exile, it follows me, reminding me that I'm nothing more than a failed son, a weak heir."

"Tarek," Freya said, taking another cautious step forward, "listen to yourself. You're letting his voice control you, even now. You don't have to prove anything to him anymore. He's gone. This trial is over."

But the flames surged higher, fueled by his resentment, by the years of pent-up anger that had burned beneath the surface, waiting for any crack to burst through. He looked down at his hands, watching as the fire pulsed, uncontrolled, a reflection of the turmoil inside him. His voice dropped, almost a whisper. "Maybe I'm no better than he thought. Maybe I'm just… destined to be this—a walking flame, destroying everything I touch."

Freya's expression softened, her voice calm and steady, a quiet strength that cut through his spiraling thoughts. "You are more than that, Tarek. But you have to believe it. Right now, the only thing stopping you from moving forward is you."

He looked up at her, the wildness in his gaze beginning to waver. "You don't understand. I… I can't control it. Not when I feel like this."

Freya took a final step closer, her hand reaching out, hovering just above his. The heat was intense, almost unbearable, but she didn't pull back. Her voice softened, barely above a whisper. "Then let me help you."

He stared at her, the flames dancing between them, his face a mixture of pain and disbelief. "Why? Why would you…?"

"Because I've seen what you're capable of," she replied, her tone unwavering. "And because I believe you're stronger than this. But you have to believe it too, Tarek. Take a breath. Find your center."

His jaw clenched, but he nodded, hesitantly drawing in a slow, shuddering breath, and then another. Freya kept her hand extended, steady and unmoving, her calm presence a grounding force against the rage and fire within him. Gradually, he felt the flames begin to ebb, retreating like waves pulling back from the shore.

With each breath, the heat lessened, the fire dimming until only faint wisps of smoke rose from his hands. He let out a long, exhausted sigh, his body sagging as if the struggle had drained every ounce of his strength.

Freya gave a slight nod, lowering her hand. "See? It's within your control. You just have to remember that."

He looked at her, the intensity in his gaze now softened, a faint trace of gratitude breaking through the lingering frustration. "You make it sound so simple."

"It's not simple," she replied quietly. "But it's possible. You're not defined by the expectations of others, Tarek. You have the power to choose what kind of person you want to be."

He held her gaze, the weight of her words settling over him. Slowly, he nodded, letting out another breath as the last of the heat faded, replaced by a strange calm that he hadn't felt in years.

"Thank you," he murmured, his voice barely audible.

Freya gave a small smile, her tone as steady as ever. "Don't thank me. Just remember this moment the next time doubt tries to take control." She turned, her gaze shifting back to the path ahead, her voice carrying over her shoulder as she moved forward. "Come on. We're not done yet."

He watched her go, a newfound respect glinting in his eyes, and after a moment, he followed, his heart lighter, the shadows of his past beginning to lose their grip.

The air around them remained thick with the fading echoes of heat and ash as they walked further along the rocky path. Tarek's breathing had steadied, and the fire within him, once a tempest of anger and resentment, simmered under newfound control. He cast a glance at Freya, who walked ahead with her usual calm stride, her expression unreadable but her presence steady and grounding. There was a strength in her silence, a resilience that seemed to have anchored him when he'd been on the verge of losing himself.

They came to a clearing where the path widened, and Freya paused, glancing back at him. She didn't say anything, but her gaze held a quiet invitation, as if giving him permission to test his newfound control, to see how far he could go with this fragile mastery of his power.

Tarek drew in a slow, deliberate breath, feeling the heat coil within him, waiting at his command. He spread his hands, focusing on the flames, imagining them not as an uncontrollable blaze, but as a steady, pulsing energy that moved with him. His fingers tingled, the warmth flowing through him like a calm river instead of a raging storm.

Freya watched, her gaze assessing but calm. "Start small," she advised, her voice even and steady. "You know the fire's there, but now it's about direction. Focus on how you want it to move, not just how much you can create."

Tarek nodded, her words grounding him as he let the flame rise slowly from his hands, a controlled glow that licked at his fingertips. He kept his focus, feeling the heat settle, no longer wild but tamed, responding to his will. The fire expanded, forming a thin, glowing barrier that pulsed softly, bending with the slightest shift of his hands.

A surge of confidence rose within him, and he glanced at Freya, a glimmer of pride in his expression. "It's… different this way. Like it's working with me, not against me."

Freya nodded, a faint smile tugging at the corners of her mouth. "Because you're respecting it. Fire is powerful, but it responds to clarity of purpose. If you focus on control rather than on force, it will move with you."

Tarek's gaze lingered on her, a newfound respect forming in his eyes. "I never thought I'd be learning something like this from an Ice Guardian. You make it look effortless."

She chuckled softly, the sound quiet but genuine. "Effortless? Hardly. It's years of training, learning to direct, to listen." Her gaze met his, and she added, "But you're more capable than you realize, Tarek. You're already starting to understand that it's not just about wielding power, but channeling it with intent."

Tarek considered her words, his mind turning over the weight of them. He had always approached his fire with the mentality of domination, trying to overpower it, force it into submission. But what Freya was teaching him was something else entirely—a balance between power and patience, a cooperation rather than a battle. For the first time, he felt the fire within him shift, almost as if it, too, recognized this new understanding.

He focused again, and the barrier expanded, forming a stable circle around him, its warmth even and steady, emanating from his hands but no longer straining against his control. He held it there, breathing evenly, feeling every pulse of energy as part of himself, his own strength guiding it without forcing it.

Freya watched, her expression softening. "Good. Now, hold that focus. Let it strengthen from within you, but don't let it slip into excess."

He closed his eyes, centering himself, feeling Freya's steady presence just beyond his circle. She was watching him, trusting him to hold his own, but ready if he needed support. Her calm steadied his heartbeat, her words echoing in his mind, and he realized that her confidence in him had been the catalyst he needed to believe in his own strength.

Opening his eyes, he let the barrier retract slowly, the flames dwindling back into his hands, leaving nothing but warmth in his palms. He looked at Freya, and his voice was quiet but filled with genuine gratitude. "Thank you. For… believing in me, even when I didn't."

She inclined her head, her gaze meeting his with a soft, unspoken understanding. "We're here to learn from each other, Tarek. And we still have a long journey ahead."

He nodded, feeling a sense of purpose and clarity he hadn't known he was capable of. He was learning that control wasn't a restraint but a direction, a focus that allowed his power to be an extension of himself rather than something that defined or controlled him.

They resumed their path, the silence between them now one of mutual respect. And as they walked side by side, Tarek knew that he had found something far more valuable than raw strength—he had found the beginning of mastery, and the unexpected guidance of an ally who, like the mountain itself, would challenge him to grow in ways he hadn't thought possible.

The heat from the trial still lingered in the air, though the flames had long faded into a quiet simmer, a faint warmth that clung to the rocks around them. Tarek stood at the edge of the chasm, his posture relaxed but his gaze distant, as if he were seeing something far beyond the shadowed path before them. Freya waited a few steps back, giving him the space to process whatever echoes still lingered in his mind, the unspoken aftermath of his encounter with the vision of his father.

She watched him in silence, the flickering torchlight casting subtle shadows across his face, softening the usual defiance in his expression. He looked different now, more vulnerable, as if he had left some part of himself behind in the flames that had tested him. And for a moment, Freya felt the impulse to speak, to ask if he was truly alright. But something held her back, an instinct that told her words would only interrupt the quiet understanding settling between them.

Tarek finally turned, meeting her gaze. There was no hint of his usual smirk, no sharp retort or sarcastic comment. Instead, his eyes held a depth she hadn't seen before, a silent acknowledgment of something shared, something understood without need for explanation.

Freya held his gaze, her own expression softening, a rare vulnerability in her eyes that mirrored his. She nodded, a small but meaningful gesture, a wordless affirmation that she'd seen his struggle and respected the strength it had taken to face it. And in that single nod, a wealth of unspoken words passed between them—a quiet acknowledgment of battles fought alone, of scars carried with pride and shame alike, and of the resilience that had brought them both here, side by side.

Tarek gave her a slight, appreciative smile, a warmth that seemed to radiate from him despite the fading embers of his trial. "I didn't think… I'd feel different," he murmured, his voice low, almost as if he were speaking to himself. "But I do. Lighter, somehow."

Freya nodded again, a small smile tugging at the corner of her lips. "It's strange, isn't it? Facing something that feels… almost as heavy as the mountain itself, and realizing it was only as powerful as we allowed it to be."

Tarek's gaze softened further, his voice almost a whisper. "I didn't think anyone would understand that. Not until now."

The silence returned, but this time it wasn't weighted with tension or unsaid accusations. Instead, it felt calm, a steady pulse that held them together as they both reflected on the trials they'd faced—both on this mountain and within themselves.

They stood there for a few more moments, neither needing to break the quiet, letting the silence speak what words could not. Freya's heart beat steadily, her own past trials feeling distant, a part of her but no longer consuming her. She realized, with a surprising clarity, that this journey wasn't hers alone. Tarek was here, fighting his own shadows, and in a way that was both humbling and comforting, they were bound by the weight they'd chosen to share.

With a final glance, Freya extended a hand toward him. Tarek hesitated, then clasped it, the warmth of his hand grounding her, their grip firm and unyielding. They released each other, the gesture enough to seal the silent bond that had formed between them, a connection forged through hardship and tempered by trust.

Without a word, they turned and continued up the path, side by side, the weight of their pasts lightened by the unspoken understanding that, whatever trials still awaited, they would face them together.

Chapter 6
The Mountain's Maze

The mountain seemed to expand endlessly around them, each step unveiling more of its haunting, forbidding beauty. Jagged cliffs rose on either side, casting long shadows across the path that twisted and narrowed, forcing Freya, Tarek, and Eirwen to walk single file. The sheer drop beside them offered a chilling reminder of the mountain's perilous design.

Freya couldn't help but glance down, her stomach knotting at the sight of the dizzying depths below. "This place… it's like a maze built to swallow travelers whole," she murmured, half in awe, half in trepidation.

"Indeed," Eirwen replied without looking back. "It was shaped by ancient forces, harsh and unforgiving. It does not care for those who walk its paths."

Tarek scoffed from behind her. "You talk like the mountain's a living thing."

Eirwen cast a knowing look over his shoulder. "In a way, it is. It tests those who pass through, revealing its paths to those it deems… worthy."

Freya frowned. "Worthy? What does that even mean?"

Eirwen's gaze turned forward again, his tone soft but firm. "It's not for us to decide. The Rift demands respect. Those who come seeking answers must tread carefully."

Tarek shook his head, his tone laced with skepticism. "You're full of riddles, you know that?"

Eirwen's lips twitched in a faint smile. "Perhaps. But riddles are often closer to truth than you think." He gestured ahead to a narrow ledge barely wide enough for one person. "Watch your step here. One wrong move, and the mountain will claim you."

Freya swallowed, steadying herself as she pressed her back to the rock face and edged across the ledge. The cold wind whipped past her, tugging at her cloak as if trying to drag her into the depths below.

"This place doesn't make it easy, does it?" she muttered, glancing at Eirwen.

"Easy paths are not meant for those seeking redemption," he replied, his tone as hard as the stone underfoot. "This mountain was never meant to comfort. It reveals only the harshest truths."

Tarek snorted as he maneuvered across the ledge, keeping his balance with a hand braced against the rock wall. "Comfort, huh? I didn't come here for comfort. But I didn't come here to get myself killed, either."

Eirwen paused, waiting for them to cross before continuing. "Then tread wisely, Firelander. The mountain does not forgive carelessness."

Freya's eyes narrowed, a chill running down her spine as she took in the twisting path ahead, where the cliffs towered and fell, each corner revealing yet another obstacle. "How much further, Eirwen?"

Eirwen's gaze scanned the horizon, his expression unreadable. "Far enough that you'll wish it were shorter. The mountain's secrets are not given freely."

Freya couldn't resist a bitter smile. "And you, Eirwen? You've seen it all, haven't you? The twists, the hidden paths… everything?"

Eirwen's gaze grew distant. "I know enough to survive, Freya. But the Rift is ever-changing. No one sees all its paths."

"Convenient," Tarek muttered, his voice dripping with sarcasm. "You lead, but you don't know where the path ends. Comforting."

Eirwen glanced back, his eyes sharp. "You're welcome to turn back. But I assume neither of you came all this way to walk away empty-handed."

Freya's gaze met Eirwen's, and she shook her head. "We're not turning back."

Tarek sighed, his voice grudgingly resigned. "Then let's keep moving. Before the mountain decides it's done with us."

As they continued forward, the mountain's landscape shifted, revealing more jagged cliffs and deep ravines that twisted away into shadow. Freya's mind raced as she tried to memorize landmarks, mentally mapping each bend, each crag, each narrow ledge that stretched before them.

"It's almost beautiful," she murmured, a hint of wonder in her voice. "Terrifying, but… beautiful."

Eirwen nodded, his gaze fixed ahead. "That's the Rift's nature. Deadly beauty. And that is why it endures."

Tarek grumbled from behind. "I'd take less 'beauty' and more stable ground."

Freya smirked, shooting him a glance over her shoulder. "Scared, Tarek?"

He shrugged, attempting to look nonchalant. "Just practical. This isn't exactly my idea of a friendly stroll."

Eirwen's voice held a note of approval. "Practicality will serve you well here, Firelander. The Rift is not forgiving to those who underestimate it."

Tarek rolled his eyes, muttering under his breath. "Trust me, I'm not underestimating anything."

Freya cast one last glance at the narrow path they had crossed, the steep cliffs and shifting shadows feeling both ominous and strangely inviting. She couldn't shake the sense that the mountain held secrets it wanted them to find—or that it wanted to keep hidden.

As they pressed on, Eirwen's words echoed in her mind: *The mountain demands respect.* And, as much as she hated to admit it, she could feel its presence pressing down on her with each step, an unyielding force that demanded her caution, her wariness… and perhaps something more.

The trio trudged forward, the mountain path shifting underfoot as the terrain gradually transformed from dense snowfall to harsh, exposed cliffs, where only a thin crust of frost clung to the jagged stone. The wind picked up, biting with a ferocity that forced Freya to pull her cloak tightly around her. The sharp gusts tugged at them, whistling through the cliffs with a keening wail that made the whole landscape feel hostile, alive.

Freya glanced back to check on Tarek, noting the strain on his face as he braced himself against the wind. His cloak whipped around him, and he clutched it tightly, his breaths coming in visible, shallow puffs that barely made it through the thin, frigid air. She slowed her pace slightly, her eyes narrowing in concern.

"You all right, Firelander?" she asked, her tone casual but with a faint note of concern.

Tarek nodded, though his face was pale, and his lips were beginning to turn a faint shade of blue. "I'm… fine," he replied, his voice tight. "Just… don't have your kind of immunity to the cold."

Freya couldn't help the faint smirk tugging at her lips. "Funny, I thought Firelanders were supposed to be resistant to all kinds of extremes."

Tarek shot her a look, half-exasperated, half-amused. "Extremes of heat maybe, not… this." He shivered, wrapping his cloak tighter around himself. "This place feels like it wants to freeze you from the inside out."

Eirwen, who had been moving ahead with a steady, unfazed stride, paused and glanced back at them. "The Rift is known for its… varying climates. It tests its travelers, forces them to adapt."

"Adapt?" Tarek scoffed, rubbing his hands together in an attempt to warm them. "Easier said than done when your fingers are turning to ice."

Freya gave him a sympathetic look, though she masked it with a touch of sarcasm. "What's wrong, Tarek? Afraid the cold might actually conquer you?"

Tarek narrowed his eyes at her. "Keep laughing, Icefolk. I'd like to see you handle a desert storm sometime."

Eirwen's voice cut in, calm and unbothered by the banter. "The mountain demands respect from all who enter its domain. You'll find no shelter from the elements here. You must simply… endure."

Freya raised an eyebrow at Eirwen. "Easy for you to say, given that you seem barely affected. How do you move through this cold like it's nothing?"

Eirwen's gaze turned distant, almost thoughtful. "Experience," he said simply. "The mountain and I... have an understanding."

Tarek gave an incredulous snort. "An understanding. Right. Maybe if it could understand that I'd rather not turn into an icicle, that would help."

Freya suppressed a smile as she watched Tarek battle the cold. Though his Firelander origins had given him a natural resilience to heat, the Glacial Rift was an entirely different realm. She noted his clenched jaw, the way he forced himself to keep pace, even as the wind seemed determined to knock him back with every step.

She matched his stride, her voice low and almost... respectful. "You know, most people from your region wouldn't have lasted this long out here. You're handling it better than I expected."

Tarek managed a weak grin. "I'll take that as a compliment, even if it sounded backhanded."

"It's not," Freya replied honestly, though she quickly masked it with her usual cool tone. "Just... an observation."

He glanced at her, his expression softening just a fraction. "Coming from you, I'll take it."

Eirwen continued to lead them deeper into the shifting landscape, where the terrain grew steeper and more unforgiving with every step. The cliffs loomed on either side, creating narrow passages that funneled the wind, making it even colder, more piercing. Freya's gaze traced the patterns of frost and ice along the rock, the way it seemed to sparkle and yet warn, as if daring them to press forward.

"Stay close to the rock face," Eirwen advised, his voice barely audible over the howling wind. "The gusts can be deadly if you're caught off-balance."

Freya nodded, falling in line, though her eyes never left Eirwen's back. She couldn't shake the feeling that he was hiding something, that his knowledge of the mountain went deeper than he let on. She glanced at Tarek, who was doing his best to follow Eirwen's advice, though he was visibly struggling with each step.

"Why'd you even come here, Tarek?" she asked, her tone half-teasing but edged with curiosity. "You know this place isn't exactly welcoming to… outsiders."

Tarek forced a smile, though his eyes held a flicker of something she hadn't noticed before—determination, mingled with something darker. "Sometimes… you have to go to places that don't welcome you to find what you're looking for."

Freya studied him, noting the weight behind his words. "You're risking a lot just to find… answers, then?"

"Aren't we all?" he replied quietly, his gaze steady as he looked at her, then shifted back to the icy path ahead.

Eirwen's voice drifted back to them, cutting through the silence. "The mountain reveals what it chooses. Those who survive its trials emerge with the knowledge they seek… or they become part of the mountain itself."

Freya felt a shiver that had nothing to do with the cold. "So that's the choice, is it? Learn its secrets… or die trying?"

"Something like that," Eirwen replied, his tone impassive. "But it's not the secrets of the mountain that should concern you. It's what it reveals within yourselves."

Tarek shook his head, his voice tinged with exasperation. "I don't need the mountain to reveal what's within me. I know myself just fine."

Freya smirked. "I wouldn't be so sure. This place has a way of… forcing things to the surface."

Tarek's gaze darkened as he pulled his cloak closer, gritting his teeth against the cold. "Well, here's hoping it can surface some warmth while it's at it."

Eirwen's faint chuckle was lost to the wind, but Freya caught the look in his eyes, a glint that suggested he knew more than he was letting on. She glanced at Tarek, his face pale with the strain of enduring the brutal cold, but she couldn't ignore the respect that flickered within her. He was far from his element, yet he pressed on, driven by something she couldn't quite name.

With a deep breath, she matched his pace, her eyes focused ahead, resolute.

The mountain air grew colder as the path narrowed, twisting deeper into the shadows. Eirwen moved ahead of Freya and Tarek, his steps precise, as though he knew every stone, every jagged edge that lined the trail. Freya watched him closely, her wariness growing with each turn they took into unknown terrain.

"Eirwen," Freya called out, her voice edged with suspicion, "how do you know this path so well?"

Eirwen glanced back, his face unreadable. "The mountain and I have an understanding," he replied smoothly. "There are paths it reveals only to those who… respect its ways."

Tarek rolled his eyes, his breath a visible puff of mist in the icy air. "Respect? This place is a labyrinth. You're leading us through it like it's your own backyard."

Eirwen smirked slightly, slowing his pace just enough for them to catch up. "You could say that. I've walked these trails before, many times."

Freya narrowed her eyes, unwilling to let him brush off the question. "And what exactly do you mean by that? This isn't just experience, Eirwen. You're moving as if the mountain itself is guiding you."

He tilted his head, his expression thoughtful. "Perhaps it is. Or perhaps I simply understand it in ways most people cannot."

Tarek huffed, his tone dripping with disbelief. "Or perhaps you're leading us in circles, and we're just supposed to trust you'll find a way out eventually?"

Eirwen gave Tarek a faint smile, unfazed. "Patience, Firelander. The mountain doesn't reveal its secrets all at once."

Freya shot him a wary glance. "Secrets, huh? And what secrets are we talking about, exactly?"

Eirwen's gaze grew distant, his voice quiet but resonant. "The mountain holds reflections… of those who tread upon its paths. Those who venture here often find parts of themselves they thought long forgotten."

"Cryptic as always," Tarek muttered, pulling his cloak tighter against the wind. "I didn't come here for soul-searching, Eirwen. I came for answers."

"And you'll find them," Eirwen replied calmly, "if you listen carefully." He gestured ahead to a narrow, winding trail that seemed to disappear into the shadows. "But understand, each path comes with its own tests. The mountain has a way of bringing our deepest fears to the surface."

Freya's gaze sharpened, a trace of unease flickering in her eyes. "What kind of tests?"

Eirwen turned to face her, his expression serious. "Doubts. Regrets. Shadows of the past. The mountain will make you face what you hide from… even if it means breaking you in the process."

Tarek scoffed, his voice laced with sarcasm. "Breaking us? That's comforting. You're really selling this path, Eirwen."

Eirwen's gaze didn't waver. "I'm not here to comfort you, Tarek. I'm here to show you the truth, whether you're ready for it or not."

Freya's jaw tightened, her mistrust deepening. "And what truth are you after, Eirwen? What do you get out of leading us through this place?"

Eirwen's expression softened, though a hint of sadness lingered in his eyes. "I once sought the same thing as you. Answers, absolution… maybe even redemption. I found what I was looking for. But I lost something, too." He looked at her intently. "I'm here to help you understand what you seek before it's too late."

Freya felt a shiver unrelated to the cold. "Too late? What are you saying?"

Eirwen's gaze was steady. "This mountain has a way of demanding more than it gives. If you're not prepared to face the truth it reveals, it can consume you. Each path, each choice, carries a cost."

Tarek shook his head, his tone defiant. "So you're saying this place… tests us? Pushes us to our limits, just for the sake of some mystical 'truth'?"

"Exactly," Eirwen replied, his voice barely more than a whisper. "The mountain strips away the layers we wear. It shows us who we truly are, for better or worse."

Freya clenched her fists, her voice filled with skepticism. "And you expect us to believe you're doing this out of the kindness of your heart?"

Eirwen's lips curved in a faint, sad smile. "Believe what you want, Freya. But I'm offering you a choice. Follow me, and perhaps you'll find what you came for. Or turn back, and you may always wonder what you left behind."

Freya glanced at Tarek, her voice low and tense. "What do you think?"

Tarek sighed, his expression grim. "I don't trust him, Freya. But… I don't think we'll get out of here without his help, either."

Eirwen inclined his head, acknowledging their hesitation. "It's not about trust, not really. It's about facing the path, together or apart."

Freya looked between Eirwen and Tarek, feeling the weight of his words settle over her. "Fine," she said finally, her voice resolute. "We'll follow. But don't think for a second that means I trust you."

Eirwen's smile was faint, almost grateful. "That's all I ask. Keep your guard up. The mountain has its ways of testing those who venture too close to its heart."

With one last wary glance, Freya motioned for Eirwen to lead. The shadows closed in around them as they followed his steps, each step echoing with a mix of curiosity and trepidation, a growing sense that they were moving closer to truths buried deep within the mountain… and within themselves.

As the last traces of twilight faded, casting a deep blue shadow over the mountain, Freya and her companions settled at a small, rocky alcove that shielded them from the biting wind. The chill remained relentless, clinging to her skin even through layers of fur, but she was thankful for any respite from the harsher elements of the day. They had been walking for hours, each step a calculated move on the treacherous trails Eirwen had chosen for them, paths that seemed to twist and narrow without warning.

Freya stretched her aching limbs, her gaze tracing the distant ridges they had crossed. The mountain stretched endlessly in all directions, a vast, unyielding labyrinth of jagged cliffs and shadowed valleys. She found herself mentally mapping the route they had taken—the steep ledges, the precarious drops, the hidden pathways winding through the rock. She tried to recall each bend, each turn Eirwen had led them through, committing every detail to memory as if the act itself might grant her some control over the mountain's vastness.

The fire crackled softly, and she caught herself staring into the flames, her mind drifting. If they failed to complete this journey, if the mountain's tests proved too much… what would it mean for her? She clenched her fists, the thought of failure twisting uneasily in her stomach. It wasn't only her life at stake; this journey had a purpose. She had left behind everything she once knew to reach this place, and there could be no turning back now, not without answers. The weight of that responsibility settled heavily on her, pushing her beyond her fatigue.

A faint movement caught her eye, and she looked up to see Tarek sitting across from her, his face set in determined concentration as he tended to the fire. Despite his obvious discomfort in the cold, he had kept up, resilient and unyielding, even when she could see the strain lining his face. Freya couldn't help but feel a reluctant respect for his endurance. The harsh elements had tested them both, and he had proved himself unexpectedly capable, his resolve as strong as the fire he carried within.

Eirwen sat slightly apart from them, his figure nearly blending with the shadows, watching the fire with an unreadable expression. Freya's gaze shifted to him, her thoughts swirling with questions she couldn't yet voice. Eirwen moved through the mountain as if it were his domain, his knowledge of the hidden paths and ancient secrets beyond anything she'd ever seen. He spoke of the mountain's will as if it were a living thing, an entity that chose to reveal itself only to those who sought it sincerely. It was unsettling, how he seemed at home in this inhospitable place, as if he were a part of the mountain itself.

Freya's voice broke the silence, her tone thoughtful. "You say the mountain reveals itself, Eirwen. But what if it decides to turn against us?"

Eirwen looked up, his eyes reflective, catching the firelight in a way that made them seem almost otherworldly. "The mountain does not turn against anyone, Freya. It tests, yes, but it does not act out of malice. Its purpose is simply to… show."

Freya's gaze didn't waver. "And if we're not ready to face what it shows us?"

Eirwen's expression softened slightly. "Then the mountain can be unforgiving. It respects strength, resilience, and, most of all, honesty. Those who lie to themselves often find its paths… difficult to navigate."

She considered his words, feeling the weight of their truth. The mountain didn't care for her doubts or fears. It demanded a kind of brutal honesty, a confrontation with the parts of herself she might otherwise wish to leave buried. The thought both unsettled and challenged her, igniting a flicker of determination to see this journey through, no matter the cost.

As the fire crackled and their shadows danced along the rock walls, Freya settled down, resting her head against her pack.

Her mind was buzzing with thoughts—questions about Eirwen's past, about the mountain's secrets, and, most of all, about her own purpose here. The silence around them deepened, the stillness broken only by the faint whisper of the wind outside their small shelter.

Just as her eyelids began to grow heavy, she glanced once more at Tarek, whose gaze had softened as he stared into the fire, lost in thought. She wondered what drove him to endure this journey, what answers he sought in these frozen heights. Their alliance was an uneasy one, yet they shared a common purpose, a shared determination to uncover something far beyond themselves.

As she closed her eyes, Freya's mind swam with fragmented images—of the mountain's winding paths, of the secrets it guarded, and of Eirwen's cryptic words. The journey stretched endlessly before them, fraught with danger and uncertainty. But as her exhaustion finally pulled her into sleep, one thought remained, solid and unwavering amidst the murk of doubts and fears:

She would push forward. She would uncover the truth hidden in these cliffs, and she would face whatever the mountain had to show her. There was no other path now.

Chapter 7
Spirits of the Past

The morning brought an eerie quiet to the plateau, where mist hung low over the ground, swirling in thin, ethereal tendrils that clung to Freya's legs as she walked. The cold here was different—a bone-deep chill that made her shiver despite her layers, the air heavy with an unexplainable weight. She couldn't shake the feeling that something watched them, an unseen presence lurking just beyond the fog.

Freya slowed her steps, her gaze sweeping across the misty expanse. "Do you feel that?" she asked, her voice barely above a whisper, almost as if she feared disturbing whatever lay in the haze around them.

Tarek, who had been walking beside her, looked up, his jaw clenched, eyes wary. "Feel it? It's like the air itself is… waiting for something," he muttered, glancing over his shoulder as if expecting to see shadows in the mist.

Eirwen, who had been leading them, stopped, his gaze scanning the surroundings with a calm familiarity. His face betrayed no surprise, as if he had anticipated this moment all along. "The mountain tests all who come here," he said quietly, his voice carrying a strange reverence. "But some trials are… more personal."

Freya felt her pulse quicken. "What do you mean, 'more personal'?" She watched Eirwen closely, hoping for a straightforward answer, though she doubted she would get one.

He looked at her, his expression thoughtful. "The mountain recognizes those who carry burdens, regrets. It reveals what lies within—what you fear most, what you cannot leave behind."

Tarek scoffed, though there was an edge to his tone, his discomfort evident. "So, we're supposed to believe that this place can… see inside us? That it's judging us somehow?"

Eirwen's eyes flickered to Tarek, a faint smile ghosting over his lips. "Believe what you will, Firelander. But this place has a way of reflecting what we hold within." He turned to Freya, his gaze steady, almost knowing. "And I think it knows why you're here."

Freya felt a chill run through her, sharper than the cold air around them. "You're saying this… this presence," she gestured to the thick mist surrounding them, "it's here because of me?"

Eirwen nodded, his expression unreadable. "The mountain has judged you, Freya. And it will reveal what it has seen, what it believes you must face."

Tarek's eyes narrowed, and he took a protective step closer to her. "And what exactly are we supposed to do about it? Just… wait here to see what it shows us?"

"Precisely," Eirwen replied, his calm unshaken. "But do not expect mercy from what you encounter."

Freya clenched her fists, swallowing the surge of unease rising within her. "And what about you, Eirwen? Aren't you supposed to be our guide?"

Eirwen's gaze softened, but he didn't move closer. "This part of the path… it's yours alone, Freya. I cannot intervene, nor would I if I could. The mountain's will must be respected."

Freya's breath misted in the air as she exhaled, her gaze fixed on the shifting fog. She could feel the presence now, heavy and cold, like a whisper pressing against her skin. It was an ancient kind of energy, powerful and unwavering, and she sensed that it had waited for her for a very long time.

Tarek shifted uneasily beside her, his hand hovering near his weapon. "I don't like this," he muttered. "We should keep moving. Standing here in the open—it's practically an invitation for something to go wrong."

But Freya held up a hand, stopping him. "No, Tarek… I need to see this through." She kept her eyes on the mist, her voice steady but tinged with uncertainty. "If this place is trying to show me something, then I have to understand it."

Eirwen nodded approvingly, his gaze almost proud. "Courage is rare here, Freya. Most would turn back."

Freya shot him a look, her voice firm. "I'm not here to turn back."

The mist thickened around her, and she felt the cold intensify, seeping through her cloak as if it sought to freeze her from the inside out. Her breaths came quicker, the air feeling heavy in her lungs. She took a step forward, feeling an invisible pull guiding her deeper into the haze.

Tarek's hand shot out, gripping her arm. "Freya, this doesn't feel right. Whatever this thing is… it's not just the mountain, is it?"

Freya shook her head, her voice barely a whisper. "No… it's something else. Something… older." She hesitated, then looked at him, her expression resolute. "But I have to know."

Eirwen's voice drifted to her, gentle yet firm. "Trust in the path, Freya. The mountain has judged you worthy of this trial."

With a final nod, she gently pulled away from Tarek's grip and stepped further into the fog. The world around her grew dimmer, the mist closing in until she felt completely alone, isolated within the embrace of the frost. And there, in the silence, she sensed it—a figure emerging from the mist, its form delicate and hauntingly beautiful, shimmering with an icy glow.

Freya's breath caught. She didn't need anyone to tell her what it was. The Frost Seraph. An ancient guardian of the mountain, a creature of legend and warning, whose presence marked those the mountain deemed in need of revelation.

The Seraph's gaze held hers, unyielding, as if peering directly into her soul. Its voice echoed in her mind, a sound both chilling and strangely comforting.

"Freya," it whispered, the word like a gust of frigid wind. "Do you carry the weight of your choices?"

Freya felt a shudder pass through her. "I… I do."

"Then show me," the Seraph intoned. "Show me the burden you carry, the truth you hide."

Freya's pulse quickened, and she took a steadying breath, meeting the Seraph's gaze with a newfound resolve. She was here for answers, for redemption—and now, face-to-face with the mountain's ancient judge, she knew she would have to confront whatever lay buried within her. There was no turning back now.

The spectral figure floated before Freya, its form woven from shimmering frost and translucent light, each movement as fluid as a winter breeze. The Frost Seraph's eyes held an intense, otherworldly gleam, and as it regarded her, Freya felt a strange mix of awe and dread. The creature embodied both elegance and power, its presence filling the misty plateau with a bone-chilling energy that seemed to dig deep into her, pulling out emotions she had buried long ago.

Freya steadied herself, forcing her gaze to meet the Seraph's. Her pulse thrummed as she struggled to maintain her composure, the weight of guilt pressing down on her, relentless and unyielding. She clenched her fists, determined not to show weakness in the face of the apparition.

The Seraph tilted its head, its voice like a whisper carried on the cold wind. "Freya," it intoned, each syllable resonating in her bones. "You stand before me, burdened by past choices. Do you come seeking redemption?"

Freya swallowed, feeling the icy tendrils of memory twist within her. "I... I came for answers," she replied, her voice steadier than she felt. "Answers about my path, about who I'm meant to be."

The Seraph's gaze remained fixed on her, unblinking and penetrating. "Answers require truth, Freya. And truth... demands sacrifice." It drifted closer, the frost in its wake crackling and snapping in the air. "Are you prepared to confront what lies within you? The shadows you fear, the guilt you carry?"

Freya felt the air grow heavier, the mist closing in as though amplifying the Seraph's presence. She forced herself to nod, fighting the urge to look away. "Yes. I am," she said, though the admission brought with it a fresh wave of unease.

Eirwen's voice drifted through the silence, calm and composed. "Face it, Freya. The mountain reveals only what it knows you are ready to see."

Freya's gaze flicked to him, noting the composed yet intense look on his face. He was watching her closely, as though this moment were a test not only from the Seraph but from him as well. Her frustration bubbled up, feeling as though she was trapped between two judges—one spectral, one silent and all too real.

The Seraph extended an ethereal hand, and with it came a vision, hazy at first but quickly sharpening with painful clarity. Freya gasped as images from her past flared to life before her eyes, each memory clearer and more intense than she had anticipated.

In the vision, she saw herself standing in the Heart Village, her home, surrounded by her fellow Guardians. She wore her Guardian cloak, pride burning in her chest as she held her spear. But then, the image shifted, twisting, and she watched as her own actions spiraled beyond her control—decisions that had seemed right in the moment, but which now carried the heavy weight of regret. She saw faces—faces of those she had failed, people she had let down when she had acted without considering the consequences.

"No," she whispered, clenching her fists. "I was doing what I thought was best… protecting them."

The Seraph's gaze held steady, unmoved. "Intentions mean little in the face of consequence. What you left behind lingers, just as the snow remains in the shadow long after the sun has risen. You left a mark upon those who trusted you, Freya. Their pain… is your legacy."

Freya's shoulders slumped under the weight of the words, and she struggled to fight back the ache of remorse that surfaced, raw and unbidden. She had thought she'd come to terms with her past, that she had moved beyond it. But here, in the presence of this ancient guardian, every failure, every moment of doubt, felt as fresh as the day it had happened.

"But I came here to atone," she said, her voice barely above a whisper. "To make it right."

The Seraph drifted closer, its icy gaze softening just slightly. "Redemption is not found in mere repentance, Freya. It is earned, step by step, as each choice shapes you. To face your past is only the beginning. The mountain's trials are far from over."

Eirwen's voice cut through again, calm but firm. "Do you understand now, Freya? The mountain does not seek to punish—it seeks to reveal. To change. Only those willing to confront themselves can truly survive here."

Freya nodded, her expression resolute despite the turmoil within. "I understand," she replied, her voice stronger this time. "And I accept it. Whatever this mountain has to show me… I'll face it."

The Seraph regarded her for a long, silent moment, the mist swirling around it as though pulled by an unseen force. Then, with a graceful motion, it withdrew, fading back into the fog but leaving behind an unmistakable chill—a reminder of the trial that had just begun.

Tarek, who had been watching in tense silence, finally spoke, his voice uncertain. "Freya… are you all right?"

She took a deep breath, nodding as she steadied herself. "I... I think so," she murmured, though her heart still pounded from the encounter. She looked back at him, offering a faint smile. "It's just... harder than I expected, facing these things."

Tarek's gaze softened, and he stepped closer, his voice quiet. "You're stronger than you think, Freya. Don't let some... mystical vision make you forget that."

Eirwen observed them with a calm, almost approving look. "The first step is always the hardest. But you've shown courage, Freya. And the mountain... it has taken note."

Freya cast one last look at the mist, feeling the weight of the Seraph's words still pressing against her chest. She didn't know what lay ahead, but the encounter had lit a fire within her—a determination to push forward, to prove to herself that she could face whatever trials awaited.

She turned to Eirwen, her expression resolute. "Then let's continue. I won't let this be the end of my journey. There's more I need to understand."

Eirwen nodded, his gaze filled with a quiet respect. "Then we press on. But remember, Freya... the mountain reveals itself only to those who accept its truths, no matter how difficult they are to bear."

Freya met his gaze, her chin lifted. "I'm ready," she said, and this time, she felt the truth of her own words.

The Frost Seraph's presence lingered, its form shifting within the mist, ethereal and haunting. Freya's heart pounded as she stared at the spectral figure, feeling her instincts pulling her in two directions—fight or flee. A part of her wanted to turn and run, to escape the icy weight of her own fears, but another part knew that running would only delay the inevitable. The Seraph was here for her, and it would not vanish until she confronted it.

"Freya," Tarek's voice broke through her thoughts, urgent and firm. "You can't just stand there. You have to fight it!"

She shook her head, her gaze fixed on the Seraph's shimmering form. "Fight it? Tarek, it's not… it's not that simple. This isn't just some enemy I can swing a spear at. It's… it's something else, something inside me." Her voice faltered, the weight of her guilt pressing down on her, binding her feet to the ground.

Tarek stepped closer, his voice a mixture of frustration and encouragement. "Freya, listen to me! You've faced worse than this. I don't know what this thing is, but I know you. You're not someone who runs away from a fight."

She glanced at him, startled by the conviction in his eyes. "Tarek, you don't understand. This isn't just about bravery. It's…" She looked back at the Seraph, her voice barely a whisper. "It's about what I've done. The choices I made, the people I hurt. This… this is all because of me."

The Seraph's gaze held hers, its voice echoing in her mind. *"Yes, Freya. You carry the weight of your choices. Do you truly believe you deserve forgiveness?"*

Freya flinched, her fists clenching as the words cut through her. She opened her mouth to respond, but the doubt choked her, leaving her silent. Tarek's voice, steady and insistent, filled the silence between them.

"Freya, you can't let it get to you like this. Whatever it is, whatever it's saying, it's just trying to make you doubt yourself. You're stronger than that."

She looked at him, her voice wavering. "Tarek, you don't understand. I failed them. I failed everyone who trusted me. And now… now I'm supposed to face that, here, with this thing?"

Tarek's eyes softened, a surprising compassion in his gaze. "Maybe you did make mistakes. But standing here, paralyzed by guilt, won't change any of that. You've come this far, Freya. Whatever this Seraph is, whatever it represents… it's just a reflection of what you already carry inside. And the only way to move forward is to face it."

Freya swallowed, feeling a surge of unexpected emotion at his words. "You really believe I can do this?"

He nodded, his tone resolute. "I've seen you fight, Freya. You don't give up. And right now, that's exactly what this thing wants. Don't give it that satisfaction."

The Seraph's voice slithered through the air, cold and probing. *"So easily swayed by words, Freya? Do you think the trust of a Firelander can absolve your sins?"*

Freya's fists tightened as she met the Seraph's gaze, a spark of defiance igniting within her. "No," she said, her voice gaining strength. "I know my past can't be erased. But that doesn't mean I have to keep running from it."

Tarek stepped up beside her, his voice steady and encouraging. "That's it. Stand your ground, Freya. Face this thing. Show it who you are."

Freya took a deep breath, her resolve solidifying. She looked at the Seraph, her expression fierce. "I may have made mistakes," she said, her voice ringing with determination, "but I am here to face them. I'm not running anymore."

The Seraph's form shimmered, as though unsettled by her newfound confidence. *"Then prove it, Guardian. Prove that you are worthy of redemption."*

Freya's grip tightened around her spear, her stance firm. "I will." She took a step forward, the weight of her guilt lifting slightly, replaced by a fierce, steady resolve. She didn't know if she could conquer the Seraph, but she knew that she wouldn't let it overpower her—not now, not when she had come this far.

Tarek watched her, a glint of pride in his eyes. "That's the Freya I know. Show it what you're made of."

With a final nod to Tarek, she advanced on the Seraph, her voice steady. "I won't let my past define me," she said, her gaze locked on the apparition. "I'm moving forward, with or without your judgment."

The Seraph's form flickered, as though reconsidering its hold over her, its icy gaze softening just a fraction. Freya braced herself, feeling both her fears and her strength colliding within her, ready to face whatever came next.

Freya's breath came in shallow bursts, her chest heaving as she stood alone in the stillness that followed the Seraph's departure. The apparition had faded into the mist as suddenly as it had appeared, leaving only the lingering chill of its presence and the ghostly echoes of her own fears. She remained rooted in place, the memory of the encounter etched into her mind, her body trembling with the weight of what had just transpired.

The silence pressed in around her, a heavy reminder of the burden she carried. Confronting the Seraph had drawn out the memories she had long buried, exposing the raw edges of her past—her choices, her regrets, and the mistakes she couldn't erase. She felt those memories like fresh wounds, the faces of those she'd failed flickering through her mind, accompanied by the hollow echoes of her own guilt. But as she replayed the encounter, the fear that had gripped her in those moments began to ease, replaced by something else—resolve.

She took a deep, steadying breath, forcing herself to focus. There was no point in running from these shadows anymore.

They were part of her, as much as her strengths and her will. And if she was to finish this journey, she had to accept them, to carry them forward without letting them define her.

Footsteps approached, and she looked up to see Tarek watching her, his expression cautious but filled with curiosity. "You okay?" he asked, his voice quiet.

Freya nodded slowly, though her mind still swam with remnants of the Seraph's haunting presence. "I'm... yes. I'm fine." She paused, choosing her words carefully. "That was... unlike anything I've faced before."

Tarek's gaze softened, a faint smile of reassurance crossing his face. "You held your ground, Freya. You didn't let it shake you."

She managed a small smile in return. "I couldn't have done it without... encouragement." Her eyes flickered with gratitude, though she kept it restrained. She was used to standing alone, but in that moment, she appreciated the reminder that not all battles had to be faced in isolation.

Eirwen, who had watched the encounter in silence from a distance, stepped forward, his face calm yet approving. "The mountain recognizes those who confront themselves with honesty. The Seraph tested you, Freya. And you emerged stronger for it."

Freya turned to him, a hard edge returning to her expression. "Stronger? It didn't feel that way. It felt like the mountain was trying to tear me apart, to make me face everything I've tried to leave behind."

Eirwen inclined his head, a faint glimmer of empathy in his gaze. "And yet, you're still standing. The mountain tests because it believes in what lies within its challengers. You have passed a threshold, Freya. One that many turn back from."

She took in his words, allowing them to settle over her. He was right. She had emerged from the encounter intact, if shaken, and the fear that had once controlled her was no longer as heavy. Instead, she felt an almost overwhelming sense of clarity, as if the doubts clouding her path had been stripped away, leaving her purpose sharper, more defined.

She looked back at the mist, where the Seraph had vanished, a final lingering chill brushing her skin. "If this is what the mountain requires… then I'll face whatever it has in store," she murmured, more to herself than to anyone else. "I won't let my past keep me from moving forward."

Tarek moved closer, a spark of pride in his eyes. "Then let's keep going, shall we? If this is what the mountain throws at us, I'd rather meet it head-on than keep waiting."

Freya straightened, feeling her determination solidify into a quiet, unbreakable resolve. She glanced back at Eirwen, whose steady gaze conveyed an unspoken respect. With a final nod, she turned away from the remnants of her encounter, ready to push forward.

The path before them lay cloaked in shadows, the mountain's secrets stretching further into the unknown. But Freya knew she would press on, not only for the answers she sought but to prove to herself that she was capable of facing whatever lay ahead, unshaken by the shadows of her past.

Chapter 8
Echoes of Regret

The entrance to the Heartstone Cavern loomed before them, half-hidden by a curtain of mist that clung to the mountain's surface like an ancient veil. The air grew thick, oppressive, charged with an energy that prickled across Freya and Tarek's skin as they approached. Shadows danced around them, the mist swirling and shifting as if alive, breathing, watching. Freya took a steadying breath, her grip tightening on her spear, feeling the unspoken promise of secrets and challenges waiting just beyond the mist.

And then, out of the shadows, a figure appeared—a slender woman draped in robes that seemed woven from the night itself, her movements silent, graceful, like the mist given form. Her eyes, pale and piercing, glowed with an ethereal light, and her presence alone commanded stillness. Freya and Tarek halted, instinctively tensing as the woman's gaze settled on them.

"Welcome, travelers," the woman spoke, her voice carrying an eerie calm that filled the silence. "You stand at the threshold of the Heartstone Cavern, but you will not pass until you have listened to the voice of Nyra."

Freya's eyes narrowed, her tone measured but firm. "Nyra… the Oracle?" The tales of an ancient seer who guarded the mountain's heart had always seemed like mere legend, yet here she was, standing in front of them, tangible and real.

The woman's lips curved into a faint smile, her gaze shifting between them. "Yes, child of ice, I am the one they call Nyra. The mountain has summoned you here, drawn by your resolve, by the fragile truce you share… and by the secrets you carry." Her gaze flickered to Tarek, a knowing gleam in her eyes. "Secrets that burn like embers, ready to ignite."

Tarek bristled, but kept his voice steady. "We didn't come here for riddles. If there's something we need to face in that cavern, let us through."

Nyra's smile widened, though her expression remained enigmatic. "So quick to charge ahead, Firelander. But not everything can be conquered with fire and will." Her gaze turned thoughtful, almost pitying. "The Heartstone Cavern is more than just a trial. It is a reflection, a place where the past speaks through the present."

Freya exchanged a wary glance with Tarek, her tone cautious as she spoke. "What do you mean, 'a reflection'?"

Nyra stepped closer, her voice lowering to a near whisper, rich with a weight they couldn't quite decipher. "In the Heartstone Cavern, every step you take will echo with the choices of those who came before you. The mountain holds memories, remnants of sacrifices made, of alliances forged… and betrayed." Her pale eyes glinted, watching Freya closely. "The trials within will test not just your strength, but your hearts, your loyalties. It will force you to confront the balance between what you desire… and what you must surrender."

Freya's jaw clenched as she absorbed Nyra's words. "Sacrifice," she murmured, a flicker of unease crossing her face. "What are you saying, Oracle? That to reach the mountain's heart, we must give up something?"

Nyra tilted her head, her gaze distant, her voice turning almost wistful. "The mountain does not ask for mere offerings, but for parts of your very self. The question you must answer is whether you are willing to pay that price."

Tarek's eyes flashed with frustration, and he took a step forward, his voice edged with defiance. "Enough of this. We didn't come here to be led in circles. If there's a path we need to take, then we'll take it. But we don't need a lesson in sacrifice from someone who hides behind riddles."

Nyra's gaze shifted to him, a hint of sadness flickering in her eyes. "You think yourself strong enough to face it alone? Then you have not yet grasped the true nature of this mountain." Her tone softened, almost a whisper. "Fire cannot survive without fuel, just as ice cannot hold without structure. You are here together, but you both cling to your own fears, your own burdens. If you do not find balance, then you will crumble. The mountain will see to that."

Freya took a deep breath, steadying herself as she looked into Nyra's eyes. "So what are you saying, then? That we have to trust each other completely? That we have to... surrender our doubts?"

Nyra nodded, her expression inscrutable, yet gentle. "The trials ahead will demand more than trust. They will demand that you let go of your fear, your pride… that you stand together as one, even if it means tearing away what you've both held tightly."

Tarek hesitated, glancing at Freya, a rare flicker of vulnerability crossing his face. "And if we don't?"

Nyra's gaze darkened, and her voice turned solemn, almost a warning. "Then the mountain will take what you will not give. The choice is yours, but the consequences are not."

A tense silence settled over them, each of Nyra's words sinking in like stones, the weight of her warning pressing on their minds. Freya and Tarek exchanged a glance, the unspoken questions and fears flaring anew between them. But Nyra's presence left no room for hesitation, her gaze holding them steady.

Freya finally nodded, her voice quiet but resolute. "We understand, Oracle. We'll face whatever lies within."

Nyra inclined her head, her expression softening. "Then go. Enter the Heartstone Cavern with open hearts, for only in unity will you withstand the trials of the past."

With a final, piercing gaze, she stepped back, dissolving into the mist as if she were part of the mountain itself, leaving Freya and Tarek alone at the threshold. The entrance to the cavern yawned before them, dark and foreboding, a silent promise of the challenges that lay within.

Tarek took a deep breath, breaking the silence. "Guess it's now or never."

Freya nodded, her gaze steely, though her mind was racing with Nyra's words. "Whatever we face in there… we face it together."

With that, they stepped forward into the darkness, leaving the world of mist and riddles behind, plunging into the heart of the mountain where the echoes of the past awaited.

As Freya and Tarek stepped deeper into the mist, the world around them blurred into shadows and whispers, the mountain's silence thickening like a shroud. And then, from the fog, Nyra appeared once more, her pale gaze fixated on them with an intensity that pierced through the gloom. She seemed to have emerged from the very stone, her movements silent, as if the mountain itself had summoned her.

Freya tensed, glancing at Tarek before turning back to the Oracle. "You again," she said, her voice guarded. "I thought you'd already given us your warnings."

Nyra's expression remained serene, but her eyes glinted with something almost sorrowful. "Warnings, yes," she murmured, her voice like the rustling of leaves caught in an icy breeze. "But the mountain's secrets run deep. I did not come to bar your path—I came to remind you of the path you tread."

Tarek folded his arms, his frustration bubbling up again. "We know what we're here for, Nyra. The Heartstone. Unity. You've made it clear enough. What more is there to understand?"

Nyra's gaze softened, shifting from him to Freya. "Much, Firelander. This journey will demand far more than physical strength, more than determination. You each hold shadows in your hearts, burdens that weigh heavy. To reach the Heartstone, you must face them together, or be consumed by them."

Freya's brows drew together, irritation mingling with unease. "We're here, aren't we? Isn't that proof enough of our commitment? We didn't come all this way just to turn back."

"Commitment is not unity, Ice Guardian," Nyra replied, her tone gentle but unyielding. "You may travel side by side, but your paths diverge in ways you cannot see. If you seek the Heartstone, you must let those paths align. It will mean sacrifice—trust that cannot waver."

Freya hesitated, the weight of Nyra's words pressing down on her. "And if we don't? What if we can't let go of... everything that's kept us here?"

Nyra's eyes flashed, her voice taking on a warning edge. "Then the Heartstone will remain beyond your reach, and the mountain will become your final resting place. It accepts nothing less than unity of spirit, a bond forged in honesty, in the laying bare of secrets. If there is hesitation, mistrust—any fracture in your resolve—the mountain will know."

Tarek's frustration gave way to unease, though he tried to hide it. "Are you saying we have to… confess everything? Bare our souls, expose every vulnerability?"

Nyra stepped closer, her gaze unfaltering. "Not to me, Firelander. But to each other." She paused, her eyes tracing the faint tension still hanging between them. "The mountain can sense fear, pride, doubt. If you seek to hide any part of yourselves from one another, it will pull those very shadows forward, and they will consume you."

Freya exchanged a glance with Tarek, unease threading through her voice. "So that's it? We have to trust each other so completely that nothing is left hidden? You ask for something… impossible."

Nyra's gaze softened, the faintest hint of compassion flickering in her expression. "Impossible? Perhaps. But you have already begun the journey toward that trust, have you not? This bond you share—it is fragile, yes, but it holds strength. You have trusted each other with your lives. This is no different. It is the heart that must yield now, not just the blade."

Tarek let out a low sigh, glancing at Freya, his voice tense but laced with reluctant acceptance. "It sounds like she's saying we need to go beyond just surviving, Freya. She's talking about something… more."

Freya met his gaze, her own expression guarded but searching. "Trust is difficult to give, especially when we don't even fully know what we're facing."

Nyra's voice cut through the silence, a final whisper that held the gravity of prophecy. "To reach the Heartstone, you must trust not only in each other's strengths but in each other's pain, each other's failures. A union of power will not be enough if your hearts remain divided."

Tarek clenched his fists, his frustration surfacing despite himself. "And what if we're not ready for that kind of trust? What if it's too much to ask?"

Nyra's face remained calm, but her eyes flashed with a strange fire. "Then you will find only stone where the Heartstone should be. But if you open yourselves to each other, if you truly merge your paths... then perhaps the mountain will offer its secrets willingly."

Freya took a steadying breath, her voice low but unwavering. "We'll do it," she said, a quiet determination in her eyes as she glanced at Tarek. "If that's what it takes, we'll find a way. But this... it isn't easy, Nyra."

The Oracle's expression softened, her voice becoming almost gentle. "No path worth treading ever is, Ice Guardian. But it is a choice only you two can make."

With those words, she melted back into the shadows, leaving Freya and Tarek alone before the entrance to the Heartstone Cavern, her warnings echoing in the stillness. They exchanged a long, thoughtful look, each seeing the uncertainty and resolve mirrored in the other's gaze.

Finally, Tarek spoke, his voice softened by the weight of Nyra's words. "I guess… it's just us now."

Freya nodded, her voice steady. "Yes. And whatever we find in there, we face it together. No secrets."

They turned toward the cavern, ready to confront the shadows that lay within—and each other's hidden truths.

Freya and Tarek moved through the mist that cloaked the Heartstone Cavern's entrance, their footsteps echoing softly in the chilled silence. Though they tried to push forward, Nyra's words lingered in their minds, heavy as the mountain's weight above them. The fog deepened, and before they knew it, Nyra appeared again, her form drifting into view like a shadow made flesh, her pale eyes glowing with an unsettling intensity.

"You carry fears that cling to you as shadows," Nyra's voice drifted around them, calm yet piercing, her gaze resting on Freya. "You, Ice Guardian, have been betrayed, cast out by those you trusted. Your heart has learned to guard itself against all else. But what does that distrust cost you?"

Freya's face tightened, her jaw clenching as she met Nyra's unrelenting gaze. "It's not distrust," she replied, a brittle edge to her voice. "It's survival. If I hadn't guarded myself, I wouldn't have made it this far."

Nyra tilted her head, her expression sorrowful yet resolute. "Perhaps. But walls built of distrust imprison as surely as they protect. How long will you carry this weight before it crushes you?"

Freya glanced at Tarek, as if searching for an answer, but his gaze was turned downward, his expression conflicted. She forced herself to take a steadying breath, her voice softer, almost a murmur. "I can't afford to let anyone in. Not completely. Trust has always been a luxury, and in my world, it only brings pain."

Tarek looked up, his gaze meeting hers with a flicker of understanding—and something more, something raw. "Freya," he began, hesitating as if choosing his words carefully. "Maybe it's not about letting anyone in completely. Maybe it's about trusting… a little, here and there, enough to share the weight." He swallowed, his own voice dropping. "That's something I've struggled with, too."

Nyra's gaze turned to him, her pale eyes narrowing as she continued. "Yes, Firelander. You, too, carry fear, but yours is of failure—a fear that claws at you, casting shadows over every choice. Your father's expectations weigh on you even now, twisting your path."

Tarek's face darkened, his fists clenching as Nyra's words hit home. "I've lived in that shadow my whole life," he said bitterly. "No matter what I do, it feels like I'll never escape it. I don't fear failure because of what it does to me—I fear it because of what it means to everyone else."

Freya's gaze softened, the sharpness of her own pain blurring as she watched him struggle. "So that's it, then," she said quietly. "You fear what your father's judgment means for you. Just as I fear what betrayal has meant for me."

Tarek glanced at her, his expression raw with vulnerability. "And how do we move past that, Freya? How do we face a trial that demands everything when we're still… still carrying all of this?"

Nyra stepped forward, her expression unyielding, her voice filled with both kindness and gravity. "To fear failure and betrayal is to fear vulnerability, yet only in vulnerability can you find the strength to let go. You are here to face these shadows, not bury them. The Heartstone will ask of you more than courage—it will ask for truth."

Freya's eyes filled with an old, deep pain, her voice faltering as she spoke. "I've seen what betrayal does. It's a poison, one that sinks into you and spreads until you can't trust yourself, let alone anyone else. If I let go… if I open myself to that again, I don't know if I'll survive it."

Tarek took a step toward her, his voice gentle yet resolute. "Freya, none of us can carry these things alone. And maybe… maybe we're here, together, because the only way forward is to face this with someone else. To face it with trust, even if it's terrifying."

Her gaze flickered, the words settling deep within her as a fragile, painful truth surfaced. "But what if trusting you… what if it leads to another betrayal? I don't think I can bear that again, Tarek."

He nodded, his voice barely a whisper. "And what if I fail you? What if I'm not enough? That's what haunts me, Freya—that I'll fall short when it matters most."

Nyra watched them, her expression softening. "To face such fears is to be vulnerable, yes. But remember, the Heartstone does not demand perfection. It asks only that you open yourselves, that you place trust in each other's hands, even with the risk of pain."

Freya looked at Tarek, her walls beginning to tremble, to loosen. "Then… then I'll try. I'll trust you, even if it's difficult. Even if it hurts."

Tarek reached out, his hand resting on her shoulder, his touch warm despite the cold mist around them. "And I'll trust you, Freya. Not because I'm fearless, but because I want to believe that there's more to this journey than shadows."

Nyra stepped back, her form dissolving slowly into the mist, her voice lingering in the air. "Let this truth guide you, and perhaps the Heartstone will show you the way forward. Unity is forged not in strength alone, but in the courage to be seen, to be known."

As Nyra vanished, Freya and Tarek remained still, each holding the weight of the other's fears, their connection stronger, fragile yet real. The path ahead waited, but they knew that now, they would face it together, carrying each other's trust as they stepped toward the Heartstone.

The mist around them began to lift, revealing the path forward, winding deeper into the mountain's heart. Freya and Tarek stood side by side, their expressions transformed, no longer clouded with suspicion or guarded distance. Nyra's words lingered in the air, the Oracle's counsel a steady pulse guiding them onward. Though their fears remained like faint echoes, they felt quieter, less oppressive, shadows rather than burdens.

Freya exhaled slowly, looking over at Tarek. "This path… it feels different now." Her voice held a sense of wonder that she rarely allowed herself, as though the mountain itself had softened, recognizing the shift between them.

Tarek gave a short nod, a glint of determination lighting his gaze. "We're not the same as we were, Freya. This place, these trials—it's asking us to step forward as something more than individuals." He paused, his tone gentler. "Together, we're stronger than either of us thought."

Freya's lips twitched into a small, reluctant smile. "For so long, I thought relying on someone else made me weak. I thought I'd lose myself in someone else's choices." She let out a quiet breath, her gaze steady on him. "But now, I see it's the opposite. Trusting you… it feels like strength, not weakness."

Tarek smiled, his expression sincere, his voice filled with a warmth that matched hers. "You know, Freya, you've taught me something, too. My fear of failure… it was like an anchor, holding me down. But realizing that I don't have to carry that alone…" He shook his head, a faint awe in his voice. "It's freeing, in a way I didn't think possible."

They shared a look, a fragile but unmistakable sense of unity sparking between them, transforming their resolve into something unbreakable. Freya adjusted her grip on her spear, her voice strong. "Then let's not waste that strength. We press forward. Whatever lies ahead, we face it together."

A surge of energy seemed to flow between them, a silent acknowledgment of the pact they had made. With renewed purpose, they resumed their ascent, their steps in sync, their strides confident. The path led them into a cavernous space, the walls alive with the faint glimmer of crystals embedded within the stone, casting a subtle light that illuminated the way.

Tarek broke the silence, his voice low but steady. "What do you think the Heartstone really is?"

Freya glanced around the chamber, her eyes tracing the patterns of the crystals. "If it's anything like Nyra described, it's not just a stone or a relic. It's a reflection, maybe even a piece of the mountain's essence. A place that mirrors what we carry inside us."

Tarek nodded thoughtfully, running a hand along the cool, crystalline wall. "So, if we come here divided, if we let our fears get in the way… it'll show us exactly that. Our failures, our doubts."

"Exactly," Freya replied, her gaze sharp. "But if we can meet it with purpose, with honesty... maybe it will show us the way through. Nyra said unity isn't just fighting alongside each other. It's about... letting go, being vulnerable." She hesitated, her voice softening. "That's not something I've ever practiced."

Tarek chuckled, though there was understanding in his eyes. "Join the club. Trusting someone else... it's not what I grew up with. But somehow, it's become... well, something I can't imagine facing all this without."

Freya's eyes softened, the smallest flicker of gratitude crossing her face. "Then we face it, every fear, every doubt, and see what the mountain has left for us to uncover."

They moved further into the cavern, and as they walked, a faint vibration began to pulse beneath their feet, as if the mountain were alive, aware of their presence. The energy intensified, filling the space, the very air around them growing heavier, charged with anticipation.

Tarek's voice broke the silence, tinged with awe. "Do you feel that? It's like the mountain... it's calling to us."

Freya nodded, a glint of determination sparking in her gaze. "Then let's answer it."

With purposeful strides, they approached a massive archway carved into the stone at the end of the chamber. Beyond it lay darkness, but instead of feeling foreboding, it seemed to invite them, a promise of clarity and truth waiting to be uncovered.

The faint glow from the crystals illuminated their path, casting shadows that twisted and danced along the stone floor.

Tarek stopped at the edge of the archway, glancing at Freya, his voice steady but infused with a hint of excitement. "Are you ready?"

Freya met his gaze, her eyes bright, her voice unwavering. "I'm ready."

They crossed the threshold together, stepping into the unknown, the air growing colder, the silence deeper. Their fears had not vanished, but they had shrunk, becoming part of the determination that propelled them forward. The mountain felt like a guardian now, its presence both formidable and welcoming, as though testing their resolve one final time.

As they moved into the cavern's depths, Freya's voice echoed softly, a murmur that carried an edge of vulnerability. "Thank you, Tarek. For standing by me… for trusting me, even when I doubted everything."

He smiled, his expression gentle, his voice barely more than a whisper. "And thank you, Freya, for showing me that strength doesn't have to be carried alone."

Together, they pressed onward, stepping into the heart of the mountain, armed with purpose and unity, their fears diminished but never forgotten, each step binding them closer as they walked toward the truth that awaited within the Heartstone's depths.

Chapter 9
Trust Forged in Frost

The path along the cliffside was narrow and unforgiving, the rock barely wide enough to support one foot in front of the other. Below, the mountain dropped off sharply into a shadowed ravine, the sound of rushing water echoing up from the depths. Freya gripped the cold stone, her fingers stiff with the chill, her breath steady as she carefully balanced on the edge. Every movement had to be measured, precise; a single misstep would be fatal.

Ahead of her, Tarek moved cautiously, his stance steady as he leaned into the cliff for support. She had seen him struggle against the cold, against the unfamiliar terrain of the mountain, yet here he was, focused and determined, pushing forward with the same resilience she herself clung to. It surprised her, how he managed to keep up, even thrive, in conditions that seemed almost designed to break him.

Freya's gaze fell to his hand as he reached back, offering her support as he navigated a particularly narrow part of the ledge. She hesitated, pride flaring at the thought of taking his help, but a sharp gust of wind nearly threw her off balance. She grabbed his hand, feeling the strength in his grip, his warmth cutting through the cold.

"Easy now," Tarek murmured, his voice calm but steady, his grip firm as he guided her across the narrow pass. "No need to test the mountain's patience."

Freya's gaze flickered up to meet his, a mixture of gratitude and reluctance in her expression. "I could have managed," she said, her voice soft but edged with defensiveness. "But… thanks."

He raised an eyebrow, a hint of a grin tugging at the corner of his mouth. "I know you could've. Doesn't mean you have to do it alone." He released her hand once she was steady, turning back to assess the next section of the path. "We're in this together, like it or not."

She watched him for a moment, a surprising warmth filling her. His words, so simple, held a sense of loyalty she hadn't expected. For all the mistrust that had plagued their journey, here, in the heart of danger, he had her back.

They moved in silence for a few more paces, each step calculated. Freya's gaze remained sharp, but her thoughts began to shift, softening her guarded view of Tarek. She had seen him at his most vulnerable, struggling against the relentless cold, and yet he remained resilient, undeterred. There was something about him—an unbreakable will, a loyalty that went deeper than mere survival instinct.

The path ahead narrowed once more, a jagged outcropping forcing them to press even closer to the rock face. Freya glanced at Tarek, her tone cautious. "This next part looks… difficult."

He nodded, his eyes scanning the edge. "Stay close. I'll go first, make sure it's solid enough." Without hesitation, he edged forward, testing the rock with his weight before motioning for her to follow.

Freya moved cautiously, feeling the strain in her muscles as she balanced on the uneven ledge. A loose stone crumbled under her foot, and she stumbled, her hand flying out instinctively. Tarek was there instantly, catching her arm, steadying her before she could fall.

"Careful," he said quietly, his voice firm but gentle. "You're strong, Freya, but even the strongest sometimes need a hand."

She took a steadying breath, her pulse quick from the close call. "I know. I just… I'm not used to relying on anyone."

Tarek gave a small, understanding nod, his gaze steady as he released her arm. "I get it. But trust isn't a weakness. Sometimes, it's the only way to make it through."

His words resonated, striking a chord within her. She nodded, feeling a small sense of relief that she hadn't expected, a loosening of the tension that had knotted her shoulders. "I suppose you're right," she admitted, a reluctant smile tugging at her lips. "Maybe I should give it a try."

They continued, the path gradually widening as they moved along the cliffside. Freya found herself paying attention to the way Tarek navigated the terrain, his steps careful yet confident. He had proven himself, over and over, his loyalty and resilience undeniable, and she felt her perception of him shift. Perhaps he was more than the fiery, stubborn Firelander she had pegged him as. There was depth there, a quality of quiet strength that she hadn't allowed herself to see before.

After a long silence, she spoke, her voice softer than before. "I can see why your people value loyalty, Tarek. It's not easy to trust others, but… you make it easier."

Tarek looked over his shoulder, a faint smile breaking across his face. "Not the compliment I was expecting, but I'll take it." His gaze softened as he met her eyes. "For what it's worth, Freya, I trust you too. Maybe we both needed a reminder."

Freya felt a warmth rise in her chest, a sense of trust settling between them like a quiet understanding. It was an unfamiliar feeling, this reluctant companionship, but she found herself welcoming it, grateful for the unexpected alliance.

They moved on, the cliffside winding toward a safer path, and though the mountain remained as treacherous as ever, Freya knew she could face it—not alone, but with someone she could finally trust, even if only tentatively.

The trail widened as they moved away from the cliffside, giving Freya and Tarek a momentary reprieve from the heart-pounding drop they had just navigated. The path was still rough, scattered with patches of ice and loose rock, but it felt solid underfoot, and Freya's tension eased slightly. She glanced over at Tarek, noting the way he pushed forward, his gaze sharp and unwavering, each step a testament to his unyielding resolve.

As they came upon a sharp incline covered in slick ice, Freya stopped, raising a hand to halt Tarek. "Wait," she said, gesturing to the icy patch. "This part can be tricky. The ice here is thinner than it looks, and the ground beneath is loose. One wrong step, and it'll slide out from under you."

Tarek studied the path, nodding thoughtfully. "Thanks for the warning," he replied, his tone respectful. "Guess you've navigated enough of these to know."

Freya allowed a small, acknowledging smile. "You learn quickly in a place like this. Or you don't last long." She glanced at him, a hint of curiosity in her eyes. "Your instincts are good, though. You don't hesitate. That's rare, especially for someone unfamiliar with the terrain."

He shrugged, a faint smile tugging at the corner of his mouth. "Guess I don't have the luxury of hesitation. Where I'm from, the land is unforgiving too—just in a different way."

She raised an eyebrow, intrigued. "Tell me about it. I've never been to the Firelands."

Tarek chuckled, the sound almost wistful. "It's… different. The heat there, it's relentless, like it's alive. Every summer, the air gets thick, and the earth cracks and buckles under the sun. Sometimes, just surviving it feels like a victory." He met her gaze, a glint of pride in his eyes. "But it shapes you, makes you tough. I guess that's why I can keep up here. You learn to adapt, no matter how foreign the challenge."

Freya nodded thoughtfully, respecting the strength that came from enduring such harsh conditions. "I suppose that makes sense. Strength through survival. There's a lot more in common between our lands than I thought." She began moving carefully up the incline, testing each step to ensure solid footing.

Tarek followed, mimicking her movements, carefully stepping where she had stepped. They moved in a rhythm, and for the first time, Freya noticed a mutual respect settling between them, each of them recognizing the resilience and capability in the other. When they reached the top, she glanced back at him, a flicker of approval in her gaze.

"You learn fast, Tarek," she said, her tone warmer than before. "And you don't shy away from the challenge. That's… impressive."

He chuckled, brushing a stray bit of snow off his cloak. "I could say the same about you. You handle this place as if you were born to it. Makes me feel like I've got a lot to learn."

Freya shrugged, a faint smile playing on her lips. "I didn't have much of a choice. The mountain demands respect, and it teaches you fast. If you're not prepared to adapt, it… takes what it wants."

They walked in silence for a moment, both absorbed in their thoughts. Freya felt the guarded wall between them begin to lower, and with it, the urge to share pieces of herself she rarely spoke about. "You know," she said after a while, her voice quieter, "I wasn't always... a wanderer on this mountain. I used to have a place, people who depended on me."

Tarek glanced at her, his eyes curious but respectful. "What happened?"

Freya's gaze grew distant, her voice tinged with regret. "I made a choice. One that... others didn't understand. They saw it as a betrayal. And so, I found myself here, alone."

Tarek nodded, his expression thoughtful. "Sometimes... people don't see the reasons behind our choices. They judge without understanding." His voice held a hint of something personal, and Freya sensed there was more to his story.

"What about you, Tarek?" she asked, her tone gentle. "Why come here, to this mountain, knowing the risks?"

He hesitated, his eyes shifting to the horizon. "I had my own reasons. There were things I needed to prove—mostly to myself. I wanted to know if I was strong enough, resilient enough. There's a lot I left behind, things I didn't want to carry anymore."

Freya nodded, feeling a kinship in their words. "Seems like we're both here to leave something behind, then. Maybe that's why we keep surviving these challenges."

He looked at her, his gaze steady and sincere. "Maybe. Or maybe we're just too stubborn to give up."

Freya laughed softly, the sound surprising even herself. "That could be it too. But whatever the reason, it's easier facing this mountain with someone who understands." She glanced at him, a faint warmth in her expression. "I didn't expect that from you, Tarek. But... it's not unwelcome."

They shared a look, a silent understanding passing between them. Freya felt a weight lift, a lightness that came with the knowledge that they were no longer just reluctant allies. Trust had formed, fragile yet resilient, born from shared experiences and quiet respect.

As they continued up the mountain, she couldn't help but feel a newfound sense of hope. The journey ahead was still treacherous, the path still uncertain, but for the first time, she didn't feel alone. And in that realization, Freya knew that whatever trials lay before them, they would face them together.

The fire crackled softly, its warmth a stark contrast to the cold, biting air that lingered just beyond their small camp. Freya sat on the ground, arms wrapped around her knees, her gaze fixed on the flickering flames. Tarek sat across from her, his silhouette outlined in the orange glow. They had made good progress through the mountain's treacherous paths, but this moment of respite brought with it a quiet heaviness. The silence between them was different now—not uncomfortable, but charged, as if both were waiting for something unspoken to surface.

Freya exhaled, her voice breaking the stillness. "I don't often talk about my past," she began, her tone low, almost hesitant. "But... I feel like I owe you an explanation."

Tarek looked up, his gaze steady, open. "You don't owe me anything, Freya. But if you want to share it... I'm here."

She managed a small, grateful smile, glancing down before continuing. "Back home, I was a Guardian. I had responsibilities, people who trusted me to keep them safe. There was a time when... when I thought I'd live my whole life serving that purpose." She paused, her fingers gripping her cloak as if to steady herself. "But I made a choice. One that... they saw as a betrayal."

Tarek's brow furrowed, his expression serious. "A betrayal?"

Freya nodded, the familiar weight of guilt settling over her. "I went against the council's orders. I thought I was protecting those I cared about, but... they saw it differently. They accused me of putting everyone at risk, of letting personal feelings cloud my duty." Her voice caught, and she took a moment to steady herself. "In their eyes, I'd betrayed my role, my people. They exiled me, stripped me of everything I once believed in."

Tarek watched her in silence, the weight of her words filling the space between them. Finally, he spoke, his voice gentle but probing. "And do you think they were right? About what you did?"

Freya met his gaze, her eyes filled with a mix of regret and defiance. "Part of me knows I was right, that my intentions were good. But there's a part that can't shake the guilt, the feeling that maybe I let them down… that maybe I was selfish." She looked away, her voice softening. "I don't know if I'll ever really forgive myself."

Tarek nodded, his gaze thoughtful. "Sometimes, the hardest thing is forgiving yourself," he murmured, almost to himself. His own expression grew distant, and Freya sensed he was grappling with his own memories.

She tilted her head, curiosity overtaking her hesitance. "What about you, Tarek? I can tell there's more to you being here than just… adventure."

He hesitated, his gaze lowering as if weighing whether to answer. After a moment, he spoke, his voice quiet, raw. "I left the Firelands because… I needed to prove something to myself. Where I'm from, there's this unspoken expectation to be strong, unbreakable. I've spent my life trying to live up to that, to show that I'm worthy of the land, the legacy we're raised with." He paused, his jaw tightening. "But somewhere along the way, I realized I was losing myself. Trying to be what they wanted, I forgot who I am, what I want."

Freya watched him, her heart softening as she caught the vulnerability in his expression. "That sounds… familiar," she said quietly. "It's hard, isn't it? Feeling like you're carrying all that weight and knowing that no matter what you do, it might never be enough."

Tarek looked up, meeting her gaze with a faint, sad smile. "Yeah. Sometimes, it feels like you're just… lost. Trying to find some version of yourself that you can actually live with."

She nodded, understanding settling between them. "It's strange," she said softly, almost as if speaking to herself. "But coming here, facing the mountain, it feels like… maybe I can find a way to make peace with that part of me. The part that I lost back home."

Tarek's gaze softened, and he reached out, placing a hand on her shoulder. "Maybe that's why we're both here. To leave behind the weight of everyone else's expectations… and figure out what we want for ourselves."

Freya felt a surge of warmth at his touch, a reassurance that she hadn't realized she needed. The silence that followed wasn't heavy with tension or regret, but with a quiet understanding. In that moment, she knew that whatever lay ahead, she wasn't facing it alone.

As they settled into the quiet of the night, Freya allowed herself to lean into the newfound trust that had begun to form between them. She didn't know what the future held, but in that moment, sitting by the fire, she felt a strange peace—an acceptance of both her past and the person beside her.

The firelight flickered, casting long shadows across the rocky walls of their makeshift camp as Freya and Tarek sat in silence, each lost in thought. The air between them held a newfound tension, a weight that wasn't born of mistrust but something more complex, something almost like kinship. Freya's eyes met Tarek's across the fire, and she took a breath, gathering the words she knew needed to be spoken.

"We're both here," she began, her voice steady but edged with a hint of skepticism, "because of what we're trying to prove. To ourselves, maybe to others. But this mountain…" She glanced toward the darkened cliffs looming above them. "It's not going to give us anything for free."

Tarek nodded, his gaze unwavering. "I know. I've come to accept that, one way or another." He paused, studying her with a measured look. "But we've made it this far together, Freya. I think it's time we decide if we're truly in this as a team."

Freya's fingers tightened around the fabric of her cloak, feeling the weight of his words settle over her. "A team?" she echoed, her tone thoughtful. "That would mean trust, Tarek. And you know as well as I do that… trust is something hard-earned."

Tarek met her gaze, his expression steady but intense. "I know. And I'm not asking you to give it easily, Freya. But out here, with everything this mountain's throwing at us, I don't think we have the luxury of hesitation. We need each other, whether we like it or not."

She felt a flicker of frustration but knew, deep down, that he was right. They'd come this far by relying on each other's strengths, by filling in where the other faltered. Freya took a deep breath, her voice soft but firm. "You're right. I wouldn't have made it to this point alone. But there's still part of me… part of me that can't just shake the feeling that this alliance could turn on me when I least expect it."

Tarek looked at her, his face open, surprisingly vulnerable. "I get it. I do. I don't trust easily either. But I'm willing to put that aside for this journey. For as long as we're facing this mountain together, you have my word—I won't let you down." His gaze softened, his voice lowering. "But I need the same from you."

Freya studied him, searching his face for any sign of deceit, any hint that he might not mean it. Yet, all she saw was sincerity, an openness that was rare and, in some ways, disarming. "A pledge of alliance, then," she said quietly, the words forming more easily than she'd expected. "No matter what this mountain throws at us, we stand together. We face it as one."

Tarek extended his hand across the fire, his expression solemn. "Agreed. No matter what happens, we face it together."

She hesitated for only a moment, then reached out, grasping his hand firmly. The fire's warmth seeped into their clasped hands, a tangible reminder of the strength they now shared. "I won't let you down, Tarek," she said, her voice filled with conviction. "Not while we're on this path."

He smiled faintly, nodding. "I believe you. And maybe, just maybe, by the end of this, we'll both find what we're looking for."

Freya let go, her gaze lingering on him as she leaned back, feeling a quiet sense of resolve settle over her. "Tell me,

Tarek… what do you think lies ahead? Do you believe the mountain will just let us walk away with what we're after?"

Tarek's smile turned wry. "Somehow, I doubt it's that simple. I don't think it's ever that simple. But as long as we're moving forward, that's all I can ask for."

She nodded, his words resonating within her. "Maybe that's all any of us can ask for. To keep moving forward, no matter what it takes." Her gaze shifted to the mountain's shadowed peaks, a glint of determination in her eyes. "Then let's do it. Let's see this through. Whatever it throws at us, we face it together."

Tarek's eyes held a warmth she hadn't seen before, a respect born from their shared trials. "Together," he agreed, his voice filled with quiet confidence.

They sat in silence for a moment, the fire crackling softly between them, the night deepening around their camp. Freya could feel a new strength rising within her, a strength that came from the knowledge that, for the first time in a long time, she wasn't alone in her journey. The mountain lay before them, filled with danger and uncertainty, but this alliance, this pledge they had forged, brought a sense of calm to her mind.

As they prepared to rest, Freya felt a glimmer of something unexpected—hope. She had been through so much, had lost so much, but here, with Tarek by her side, she felt the faint stirrings of a future she had thought she'd lost. She closed her eyes, the weight of their pledge settling over her like a shield, as she embraced the strength of their newfound alliance, ready to face whatever trials awaited them.

Chapter 10
Shadows of Doubt

The path was treacherously narrow, flanked by steep cliffs on one side and an unyielding wall of stone on the other. Freya and Tarek moved cautiously, their eyes scanning the shadows, instincts sharp from the trials they had already faced. But just as they rounded a bend, a low, menacing chuckle echoed through the air, halting them in their tracks.

"Ah, Tarek," came a gravelly voice, heavy with derision. "Didn't think I'd find you in a place like this. Looks like I'm lucky after all."

Freya and Tarek turned to see a tall, armored figure emerge from the shadows. He stood with a brutal confidence, a wicked grin spreading across his face as he regarded them, his sword gleaming ominously in his hand. Freya instinctively tightened her grip on her spear, stepping protectively closer to Tarek.

"Haldor," Tarek muttered, his expression darkening. "I should've known they'd send someone like you."

Haldor smirked, his gaze sharp and calculating. "When there's a hefty price on someone's head, I'm bound to show up eventually. It's just business, you understand."

Freya shot a questioning look at Tarek. "A bounty? For you?"

Tarek clenched his jaw, his eyes still locked on Haldor. "I'll explain later. Right now, we need to deal with him."

Haldor laughed, taking a step forward, his boots crunching on the frosty ground. "I'd listen to your friend, Guardian," he sneered. "You don't know who you're dealing with. Step aside, and I'll make this quick for him. I'm sure you'd rather avoid unnecessary pain."

Freya lifted her spear, her expression unyielding. "You're mistaken if you think I'm letting you lay a hand on him."

Haldor raised an eyebrow, clearly amused. "You'd protect him? Really? You must be more foolish than you look, girl. He's nothing but a liability."

"Say what you want, Haldor," Tarek shot back, his voice calm but edged with steel. "But if you're coming after me, you'll have to get through both of us."

"Oh, believe me," Haldor sneered, his grip tightening on his sword. "I've handled worse than a pair of amateurs. This will be over in a heartbeat."

Freya's eyes flashed with defiance as she took her position, her stance steady beside Tarek. "We're no amateurs. And you'll regret underestimating us."

Without another word, Haldor lunged, his massive blade slicing through the air with lethal precision. Freya and Tarek moved in unison, their instincts guiding them as though they shared one mind. Freya blocked Haldor's strike with her spear, her movements quick and fluid, each deflection creating an opening for Tarek to strike from the side.

"Think he's figured out he's outmatched yet?" Tarek muttered, ducking under another swing and sending a burst of fire toward Haldor's feet.

"Not a chance," Freya replied, her voice steady, her eyes focused on every shift of Haldor's stance. "Arrogance blinds people like him. Let him make mistakes."

Haldor grunted, his expression twisting in frustration as he parried Tarek's fiery attack and swung his blade toward Freya. "You two think you're clever, don't you?" he growled. "I've been at this a long time—too long to fall for some childish tricks."

Freya met his strike with a fierce parry, her voice cold and controlled. "Then maybe it's time you retired."

Tarek grinned, his eyes bright with determination. "Besides, Haldor, I'd say our 'childish tricks' are working pretty well."

Haldor's frustration deepened, his strikes growing more forceful, but his precision waned as he struggled to keep up with their relentless coordination. Freya and Tarek moved with perfect timing, each attack and defense flowing naturally, their synergy forming a shield that Haldor couldn't break.

Finally, Haldor stumbled, and Freya took advantage of the moment, sweeping his legs out from under him with her spear. He crashed to the ground, his sword clattering to the side. She pressed the tip of her spear to his chest, her voice calm and unyielding.

"This is over, Haldor. Leave, while you still can."

But Haldor only laughed, though his voice was weaker, pained. "You think I'll give up that easily? I'll be back, Tarek. And I won't come alone next time."

Tarek stepped forward, his voice steady and resolute. "Then we'll be waiting. But know this—no bounty, no amount of money will protect you if you cross us again."

Haldor's gaze darkened, but he nodded grudgingly. "Fine. You win today." He pushed himself up, casting them both a look of pure malice. "But this isn't over."

He turned and disappeared into the shadows, his footsteps fading into the mountain's silence. Freya and Tarek stood motionless for a moment, the tension slowly dissipating, leaving only the faint echo of their breaths in the cold air.

Finally, Tarek let out a shaky laugh. "Well… that was exhilarating."

Freya smirked, lowering her spear. "Exhilarating? I'd call it a close call. You have some interesting enemies, Tarek."

He met her gaze, a hint of admiration in his eyes. "Maybe. But with you by my side… I think I can handle them."

She held his gaze, a warmth settling between them, an unspoken acknowledgment of the strength they shared. "Then let's keep going. Whatever comes next, we face it together."

They turned, side by side, their bond stronger, their trust fortified by the battle they'd just fought. As they continued along the path, each step held the quiet certainty that no force could shatter the unity they had forged.

The mountain pass narrowed further as Freya and Tarek pressed forward, their breaths forming clouds in the biting air. The silence around them was a stark contrast to the recent battle with Haldor, but the tension lingered, an undercurrent neither could ignore. Freya cast a quick glance at Tarek, a hint of relief flashing in her gaze. They'd faced down Haldor together, forged an even stronger bond in the heat of the fight. But there was something unsettling about the calm that followed, as though the mountain itself were holding its breath.

Then, from nowhere, a shadow flickered—a streak of dark steel cutting through the air. Freya only had time to shout, "Tarek! Move!"

But her warning came a heartbeat too late. Tarek turned just as a second blade slashed across his side, the impact sending him stumbling back, his hand clutching his side as he collapsed against the rocky ledge, gasping in pain. Blood seeped through his fingers, dark against the snow.

"Tarek!" Freya's voice trembled, her heart pounding as she dropped to her knees beside him, her hand reaching for his. "Stay with me. We're not done here."

He winced, his jaw clenched, attempting a weak smile. "Guess I got a little… careless," he managed, his voice strained.

"Don't you dare joke about this," she whispered, her voice laced with fear she could barely control. "Just hold on. I'm going to get you out of here."

But as she looked around, Freya's heart sank. The mountain path had become a narrow ledge, the steep cliffs offering no escape from the blizzard that had begun to roll in again. She could feel the icy wind biting at her skin, the chill amplifying the urgency of their situation.

Tarek's hand tightened on hers, his voice a murmur, weaker now. "Freya… if you have to go, you should. Save yourself. Don't—"

"No," she cut him off, her voice fierce, her gaze unwavering. "I'm not leaving you, Tarek. I made a choice, remember? To trust you, to stand by you. I'm not going back on that now."

He looked up at her, surprise mingling with gratitude, his voice barely above a whisper. "Freya… I don't want you to risk everything for me."

Her jaw tightened, her eyes fierce as she met his gaze. "It's not a risk. It's a choice. And I'm choosing you."

Despite the pain, Tarek managed a faint, broken smile. "You're as stubborn as this mountain."

"And you're as reckless as a wildfire," she replied, a tremor in her voice as she held his gaze. "But you're my wildfire."

The cold intensified, the blizzard swirling around them, threatening to engulf the narrow ledge. Freya's heart pounded, a fierce determination rising within her. She looked around, her mind racing as she tried to find a way to shelter them both from the storm. But there was only one option—the cliffside had a small overhang, a rocky alcove just large enough to shield Tarek if she could reach it in time.

"Hold on, Tarek," she murmured, wrapping her arm around his shoulders and pulling him to his feet, bearing as much of his weight as she could. His breaths came in shallow gasps, his face pale, but he didn't protest, leaning into her strength.

"Freya, you don't have to—"

"Quiet," she whispered, her voice strained but resolute. "We're getting through this. Together."

Each step was a struggle, the biting wind making her footing treacherous as she guided him toward the alcove. Tarek's weight pressed heavily on her, but she refused to falter, her focus unyielding. As they reached the shelter, she eased him down gently, her hands trembling from both exhaustion and the cold.

She knelt beside him, her voice soft but filled with urgency. "You're going to be fine, Tarek. I'll keep watch."

He looked up at her, his gaze filled with something deeper than gratitude, a warmth that defied the blizzard surrounding them. "Freya... I don't deserve this."

Her hand found his, gripping it tightly. "You do. More than anyone I know."

For a long, silent moment, they simply held each other's gaze, the storm raging around them but forgotten in the intensity of the connection between them. Freya felt something shift within her, a realization that went beyond loyalty or trust—something she'd tried to deny, but could no longer ignore.

"I chose you," she whispered, her voice barely audible over the wind. "And I'd do it again. No matter the cost."

Tarek's expression softened, his eyes shining with something unspoken. He gave her hand a weak squeeze, his voice a murmur. "Then I'll fight too. I'm not letting you face this alone."

She smiled, her resolve solidifying even further as she huddled beside him, shielding him from the storm. Whatever the mountain demanded of her, whatever trials lay ahead, she knew now that her strength came not from standing alone, but from standing beside him, each choice a testament to the bond they had forged against all odds.

And together, they braced themselves against the night, knowing that their shared strength was the only thing that could see them through.

The blizzard's fury intensified, and within the swirling snow, the menacing silhouette of Haldor reappeared, his shadow growing darker, more ominous. His grin was savage, eyes gleaming with satisfaction as he stalked forward, confident that Tarek's injury had left them vulnerable. Freya could feel the raw fear twist in her stomach, but she pushed it down, her gaze hardening as she positioned herself protectively between Tarek and Haldor.

"Well, well," Haldor sneered, his voice cutting through the howling wind. "Looks like you're weaker than I thought, Firelander. And here I'd worried you'd put up a real fight."

Tarek struggled to sit up, his face pale, but his eyes burned with defiance. "I'm not done yet," he rasped, though his voice trembled with the effort.

Freya held out a hand to steady him, her tone fierce. "Haldor, if you think we'll just lie down and let you take what you want, you're wrong. You don't understand what we're capable of."

Haldor chuckled, lifting his sword with a cruel smile. "Please, don't flatter yourself. I know exactly what you're capable of—limited tricks, parlor games. I'm the one with real power here."

Freya's hand tightened around her spear, her voice low and steady. "You have no idea what we're capable of."

As she spoke, a surge of energy coursed through her, resonating with something deep, something tied to the core of who she was—and who Tarek was beside her. Tarek felt it too; his eyes widened as their powers stirred together, a force neither had ever experienced, like two currents pulling into a single, roaring wave.

Tarek looked up at her, realization dawning. "Freya… do you feel that?"

She nodded, the intensity of their bond resonating with every heartbeat. "Yes. I think… I think we can use this. Together."

Haldor sneered, his eyes narrowing. "Enough of your theatrics. I'm taking that bounty, and I'll leave your bodies for the crows."

But Freya and Tarek shared a silent look, a trust born of countless battles and deeper than words. They took each other's hand, and a surge of raw, elemental energy erupted between them, their combined power swirling in a whirlwind of flame and frost.

Haldor took a step back, his confidence faltering. "What… what is this?" he spat, struggling to mask the fear creeping into his voice.

Freya's gaze turned icy, her voice laced with an authority that even she hadn't known lay within her. "This, Haldor, is the strength you could never understand. It's not just power—it's unity. And it's more than enough to end this."

Together, they raised their free hands, their bond surging like a storm. Frost and fire merged, the freezing chill mixing with blazing heat, creating a swirling tempest that crackled with raw energy. Snowflakes burst into steam as their powers intensified, forming a barrier that pushed Haldor back, his smug expression replaced with genuine panic.

"Impossible!" he shouted, raising his sword in desperation. "You're nothing but children with illusions of grandeur!"

Tarek met his gaze, his voice unwavering. "And yet, it's enough to stop you."

With a fierce shout, they unleashed their combined energy, the full force of fire and ice crashing toward Haldor in a swirling vortex. The elemental storm engulfed him, tearing the ground beneath his feet and forcing him to his knees, his sword clattering from his grasp. He cried out, his voice lost in the roar of the tempest as he struggled to withstand the power bearing down on him.

Freya and Tarek pushed harder, their hands still clasped, each drawing strength from the other, their energies in perfect harmony. Haldor's cries faded, his figure barely visible within the raging storm until, with one final surge, they unleashed the full extent of their power. The storm exploded outward, flinging Haldor backward, his body crashing against the cliffside and slumping, motionless, to the ground.

As the energy dissipated, the blizzard quieted, leaving the mountain eerily silent in the aftermath. Freya and Tarek stood together, their hands still linked, breathing heavily, their bodies trembling from the force of what they had just unleashed. But as the surge of power faded, exhaustion washed over them like a tidal wave.

Tarek staggered, his grip loosening, his voice weak. "Freya… I don't think… I can…"

Freya's vision blurred, the world swaying around her. "I… I know. I'm just as…"

Before she could finish, her knees buckled, and she felt herself collapse beside him, the world spinning as darkness crept in at the edges of her vision. She tried to hold on, to stay conscious, but the battle had taken everything they had. The last thing she saw was Tarek beside her, his eyes closing as he, too, succumbed to the exhaustion.

And then, everything went black, their bodies lying still on the frozen ground, side by side, as the mountain watched in silence.

The air around them was still, almost reverent, as if the mountain itself were acknowledging what had just transpired. Freya stirred first, the cold seeping through her limbs a stark reminder of the toll their battle had taken. She pushed herself up slowly, her vision swimming as her body fought to regain its strength. Beside her, Tarek lay still, his breathing shallow, his face pale but peaceful. She reached over, her hand trembling as she shook his shoulder gently.

"Tarek… wake up," she whispered, her voice hoarse.

He stirred, a low groan escaping his lips as he blinked against the light. Slowly, he turned to her, a faint, exhausted smile breaking through. "Did... did we do it?" His voice was barely a whisper, each word laced with fatigue.

Freya nodded, managing a weary smile. "We did. Haldor... he didn't stand a chance." She looked over to where his fallen form lay at the base of the cliff, motionless, their combined power having rendered him a mere shadow against the snow.

Tarek pushed himself up on his elbows, his gaze following hers, and he let out a shaky laugh. "Well, that's one way to settle things." He fell silent, his expression darkening as the weight of their victory settled on him. "But... Freya, did you feel it? The power—it was like nothing I've ever known. But it... it took everything."

Freya's eyes softened as she met his gaze, a mixture of awe and unease reflecting in her expression. "Yes, I felt it. It's as if our powers combined... but at a cost. I've never felt so drained." She hesitated, her voice lowering. "And it wasn't just physical. It was like part of myself... slipped away."

Tarek's brow furrowed, his gaze thoughtful. "Do you think... our connection, this bond we share—could it be... dangerous?"

She looked down, her hands clenched tightly in her lap. "I don't know, Tarek. I thought our bond was our strength, that together we could face anything. But now..." She trailed off, struggling to find the words. "Now I wonder if we're tempting something far more powerful—and uncontrollable—than either of us can handle."

He placed a hand over hers, grounding her, his voice steady despite the uncertainty in his eyes. "Freya, we survived. We fought, we won. Yes, it was draining, but we're here. Together. Doesn't that count for something?"

Freya let out a slow breath, meeting his gaze, her voice soft but laced with a vulnerability she rarely allowed. "Yes, it does. But what happens the next time we're forced to use that power? Will it cost us more than just our strength?"

Tarek looked away, his expression troubled. "It felt limitless… and that's what scares me." He looked back at her, his eyes searching. "Do you think this connection… this power we have, is meant to bring peace? Or… could it lead to something darker?"

She swallowed, feeling the weight of his words. "I've always believed in balance, Tarek. That power—especially power this immense—demands a balance. I want to believe we can use it for something good. But I can't ignore the risk that it could consume us, just as easily as it consumed Haldor."

They sat in silence, the echoes of their battle lingering in the air. Finally, Tarek broke the stillness, his tone softer, more contemplative. "Then we make a promise—to each other. That no matter what happens, we don't let this power define us. That we hold on to who we are, even if it means sacrificing the bond when it's necessary."

Freya's gaze flickered with a mixture of sadness and resolve. "Are you saying… we'd have to let go of this connection if it becomes too dangerous?"

Tarek nodded, his voice somber but resolute. "If it means protecting each other, protecting everyone… then yes." He reached out, taking her hand firmly in his. "Freya, this power, this bond—it's a part of us, but it doesn't have to control us. If it comes to it, we have to be willing to let go."

She held his gaze, her heart heavy with the gravity of his words, yet strengthened by his conviction. "Then I promise," she whispered, her voice steady. "If the day comes that our bond risks more harm than good, I'll let it go. I'll choose the peace we've fought so hard for, over the power that could destroy it."

Tarek squeezed her hand, a faint, weary smile crossing his face. "Then let's make that day never come."

They sat together in the quiet aftermath, their hands still intertwined, each absorbing the weight of their decision, the silent promise now binding them as much as their shared power. The mountain was silent, its icy air still and solemn, as though recognizing the balance they had struck within themselves—a balance as fragile as the bond that connected them.

And as they rested, side by side, Freya felt a tentative hope settle within her. They had faced the mountain's fury and their own fears, emerging stronger yet aware of the delicate line they walked. For now, that was enough.

Chapter 11
The Hidden Path

The air grew colder as Freya and Tarek continued their climb, the weight of the mountain pressing down on them, a silent but powerful force that seemed to know every weakness, every crack in their armor. They moved in a cautious rhythm, each step slow and deliberate, conserving the strength that had already been pushed to its limits. The mountain's silence felt heavier, more intense, as if it were holding its breath, waiting for the moment to test them once more.

Freya's breath fogged in the cold, her gaze fixed on the path ahead. But as she took another step, a familiar shape appeared in the mist before her—a figure shrouded in shadow, yet unmistakable. She stopped abruptly, her heart tightening as Elder Iska's face came into focus, his gaze piercing, carrying the weight of a thousand memories and regrets.

"Freya," his voice echoed, steady and cold, like the mountain air itself. "Do you remember the day you were cast out? The pain in your heart, the bitterness? You think you can bury it here, in the snow and ice?"

She swallowed, her voice barely a whisper. "You're... you're not real." But the words rang hollow, for the vision was sharper, clearer than any memory, and the sting of her exile felt as fresh as the day it had happened.

"You still seek to prove yourself," the apparition continued, his voice laced with a hint of disdain. "As if strength alone could atone for what you failed to protect. As if all of this would change the past."

Freya clenched her fists, her voice growing steadier, but filled with an old, familiar pain. "I was betrayed. Left with no choice, cast aside by the very people I trusted. I did what I could, what I had to."

The figure's expression remained impassive, his voice a cutting whisper. "Is that what you tell yourself? That betrayal was inevitable? That you bore no part in it?"

Freya's gaze darkened, but her voice softened, as though she were speaking to the vision and herself at once. "Maybe I was too trusting. Maybe I believed too easily in people who only saw my loyalty as a weapon to wield. But I am stronger now. I won't be betrayed again."

The image flickered, Elder Iska's face fading into mist as the mountain's silence returned, a haunting emptiness that seemed to echo her words.

Meanwhile, Tarek moved a few steps ahead, his eyes focused on the path yet wary, as if expecting the mountain to reveal its next trick. But as he stepped forward, he felt an oppressive weight settle on him, a voice he knew too well filling the stillness around him.

"Tarek," the voice was sharp, authoritative, the tone of a man accustomed to obedience. His father's voice. "Is this what you've become? A deserter, a vagabond clinging to lost causes? This is what you left your home for?"

Tarek stopped cold, his breath catching. He turned, half-expecting to see his father's shadow standing behind him, that disapproving gaze, the familiar sneer. But there was no one there—just the relentless mist, thick with memory.

He clenched his jaw, forcing himself to stay steady, his voice low. "I left to find my own path. To fight for something that matters, not just to follow your orders, to be another pawn in your plans."

His father's voice echoed, harsh and biting. "You were given power, purpose, everything you needed to succeed, yet you cast it all aside. For what? A lost cause? A stranger's approval? Or perhaps it's for this girl you've tied yourself to—yet another miscalculation."

Tarek's fists clenched, the words cutting deeper than he wanted to admit. "Freya is stronger, more honorable than anything you could understand. And I'm not a failure for trusting her, for choosing a path you never had the courage to walk."

The voice seemed to waver, but the disdain lingered. "Strength fades, Tarek. Loyalty wavers. And trust…" His father's voice faded into a bitter laugh. "Trust is a luxury for those without ambition. Remember that."

The silence returned, leaving Tarek standing alone, his heart pounding, the remnants of his father's words echoing in his mind. He turned, catching sight of Freya, who was looking down, her face shadowed by a similar, haunted expression. She glanced up, and for a moment, their gazes met, each seeing the traces of pain reflected in the other.

"Freya," Tarek's voice was quiet, almost tentative. "Did you… did you see something, too?"

She nodded, her gaze distant, a faint tremor in her voice. "It was Elder Iska. He reminded me of… of what I failed to protect. What I lost because I trusted too easily."

Tarek let out a slow breath, his tone filled with a rare understanding. "I heard my father's voice. He told me I was wasting my life… that trusting you was a mistake."

Freya's eyes softened, a flicker of sadness mixed with defiance. "They're testing us. The mountain knows our weaknesses, our fears. But it's just shadows, Tarek. Nothing more."

He nodded, forcing a reassuring smile, though a lingering doubt remained in his gaze. "You're right. But these shadows… they feel real enough to haunt us. We just have to keep moving forward."

She took a steadying breath, her voice stronger, filled with a quiet determination. "Yes. We've faced too much to let ghosts stop us now."

With a final glance at each other, they resumed their climb, the unspoken weight of their pasts pressing down on them. But their steps were firmer, their shared purpose a shield against the shadows of doubt and memory that lingered around them. The mountain watched, its silent warning ringing in the air, but together they pushed onward, resolved to face whatever lay ahead, bound by a trust that no apparition could break.

The mountain's path led them to a narrow ledge where the wind howled past, biting cold and relentless. But Freya and Tarek had fallen into a heavy silence, the echoes of their visions lingering around them like shadows that refused to fade. Each step felt like an anchor pulling them down, their unspoken fears hanging in the air between them.

Finally, Freya stopped, pressing her hand to the rough rock beside her, her gaze fixed on the frozen ground. "Tarek," she began, her voice barely more than a whisper, though steady. "What did your father say to you… in that vision?"

Tarek hesitated, his eyes distant as he glanced away, his voice low. "He reminded me of all the things I left behind. Told me that I'd… failed." He swallowed, his voice bitter. "He said I was wasting my life here, that I was weak for… for trusting you."

Freya flinched at his words, though she kept her expression guarded. "And… do you believe him?" Her voice was calm, but a vulnerability trembled beneath the surface.

Tarek looked at her, his eyes filled with a mixture of regret and something deeper, something he'd kept hidden for far too long. "I don't know. Part of me feels like… maybe he's right. I mean, leaving home, walking away from everything I knew—it made me feel like I was running from something. And trusting someone—anyone—felt like a mistake. Like I was asking for disappointment."

Freya's gaze softened, a faint sadness in her eyes. "You're not alone in that. I spent so long convincing myself that trust was a weakness, that letting anyone close would only bring pain." She took a breath, her voice barely steady. "Elder Iska... he was like a father to me. He trained me, guided me, and in the end, it was all taken away because I believed in people who betrayed me."

Tarek's expression grew somber, understanding flickering in his gaze. "But you kept going. Even after everything... you chose to keep fighting."

She gave a bitter laugh, her voice tinged with both sadness and pride. "Fighting is all I know. But now..." She paused, looking at him with a hesitant, almost fragile expression. "Now, I don't just fight for myself. Somewhere along the way, I started fighting for you too."

He held her gaze, something raw and vulnerable shining in his eyes. "Freya... I don't know if I deserve that. I left my family, my people, because I was afraid. Afraid that I'd always be nothing more than his pawn, a tool in his schemes. When I saw you... someone who fought for her own path... it terrified me, but it also made me realize what I was missing."

Freya's expression softened, her voice quiet but resolute. "Maybe that's why we found each other. Two people who thought trusting anyone else would be their undoing. And yet here we are… trusting each other, against all odds."

Tarek laughed softly, though there was a trace of pain in his voice. "And somehow, it feels like the most terrifying thing we've faced on this mountain."

She nodded, a faint smile tugging at her lips. "Yes. But also… the most freeing."

They stood in silence for a moment, the harsh wind a distant roar as they shared this rare, unguarded moment. Freya took a breath, a new determination flickering in her eyes as she looked at him, her voice steady yet soft. "Tarek, whatever happens… I want you to know that trusting you wasn't a mistake. Maybe I've made mistakes in the past, but this—" she gestured between them, a faint vulnerability in her gaze, "—this isn't one of them."

Tarek's eyes softened, and he took a step closer, his voice quiet but sincere. "Thank you, Freya. For giving me a chance when I didn't even believe in myself. For… letting me be someone you could trust."

She gave a small, almost shy nod, her guard lowering further than she ever thought possible. "And thank you… for showing me that strength isn't just in fighting alone. That maybe, just maybe, trusting someone can make us stronger than we ever were."

He smiled, his gaze warm. "So… we keep going. Together. Even if it means facing more of our pasts, more of our fears."

Freya nodded, her voice filled with a quiet, newfound strength. "Yes. Together. Whatever shadows the mountain throws at us, we face them. And maybe, by the end of it, we'll come out stronger... whole."

They stood close, the unspoken promise between them deeper than words, a bond forged in both strength and vulnerability. And as they resumed their climb, they carried with them not just their own strength, but the strength they had found in each other—a strength that no vision, no shadow, could ever break.

The path steepened as they climbed higher, the chill in the air sharper, more biting. Freya and Tarek moved carefully, side by side, but with a different energy than before—a calm resilience underpinned by a strength born from vulnerability. Each shared word, each quiet confession, had lightened the burdens they carried, and now, with every step, a silent determination bound them.

The trail narrowed further, leading them to a small plateau bathed in the dim glow of the evening light. The space was quiet, a pocket of calm amid the mountain's harsh terrain, almost as if the mountain itself was offering them a moment to gather their strength. Freya paused, her gaze drawn to the vast sky above, the stars beginning to emerge, shining faintly against the deepening dusk.

"We're close, aren't we?" she murmured, her voice soft.

Tarek nodded, following her gaze. "Yes. The Heartstone's summit is near." He hesitated, then turned to her, his expression thoughtful. "Freya… before we go any further, there's something I need to say."

She looked at him, curious but patient. "Go on."

He took a deep breath, his eyes filled with a quiet resolve. "I know we've faced a lot to get here. We've fought together, protected each other, and you… you've trusted me more than I ever thought anyone would. And I want you to know that, whatever happens when we reach the Heartstone, I'm with you. I won't turn back. Not for anything."

Freya's gaze softened, a faint smile playing on her lips. "I feel the same way, Tarek. For so long, I thought strength was something I had to carry alone. But you've shown me that strength can be shared. That it's… even stronger when it's shared."

They held each other's gaze, the quiet words they'd shared over the past few days weaving together into something unspoken yet undeniable. Freya took a step closer, her voice steady. "Tarek, if we're going to reach the Heartstone, we need to do it as one. We can't have doubts, can't let fear break us apart. Not now."

Tarek nodded, his expression serious. "Then let's make it official." He extended his hand to her, palm up, his gaze unwavering. "An oath, Freya. Here, on this mountain, before we face whatever trials the Heartstone has for us. We swear to each other that we'll see this through. Together."

Freya looked down at his outstretched hand, her heart pounding with the weight of his words. She felt the solemnity of the moment settle over her, each word resonating deeply. Without hesitation, she placed her hand in his, their fingers entwining, a promise spoken without a single word.

She met his gaze, her voice soft but filled with fierce determination. "I swear it. No matter what the mountain demands, no matter what I have to give up… I'll stand by you, Tarek. I won't abandon you."

Tarek's grip tightened on her hand, his voice low but equally resolute. "And I swear the same, Freya. I'll protect you, stand with you, even if it costs me everything. This isn't just about reaching the Heartstone. It's about trusting each other, choosing each other… no matter the price."

The words settled between them, an unbreakable vow forged in the mountain's silence, binding them in a way that transcended friendship, or even loyalty. Freya felt a warmth rise within her, a strength unlike any she'd ever known. The fear, the doubt, the weight of her past—they all felt lighter, as if the mountain itself had lifted them away, leaving only a fierce, unwavering resolve.

She looked down at their joined hands, then back up at him, a soft smile tugging at her lips. "Then it's decided. No turning back."

Tarek returned her smile, a warmth in his gaze that softened the harshness of the mountain around them. "No turning back," he echoed.

They stood there in silence, the weight of their oath lingering in the cold air, grounding them, binding them in purpose and in spirit. Freya felt her heart steady, the certainty of their unity fueling her with a newfound strength. Whatever trials awaited at the Heartstone, she knew now that she would face them without fear, without doubt—because Tarek was beside her, bound by the same resolve.

Finally, she released his hand, her gaze fixed on the path ahead. "Then let's go," she said, her voice filled with quiet confidence. "Together."

Tarek nodded, his own determination reflected in his eyes. "Together."

They turned toward the mountain's peak, their steps in sync, each stride carrying the weight of their oath and the strength of their bond. And as they ascended, the stars above seemed to shine brighter, as if bearing witness to their vow, illuminating the path toward the Heartstone and whatever destiny awaited them there.

The final stretch of the path was steep, winding upward in tight switchbacks that clung to the mountain's edge, each step a test of balance and resolve. Freya and Tarek moved cautiously, their breaths turning to mist in the cold, thin air. The silence was profound, broken only by the crunch of their boots against the frostbitten stone. They climbed together, their recent oath a silent drumbeat in their minds, steady and unwavering.

As they rounded a bend, Freya paused, her eyes narrowing as something flickered in the distance. At first, she thought it was just another glint of starlight off the ice, but this was different—steady, warm, and faintly pulsating, like a heartbeat.

"Tarek," she whispered, her gaze fixed on the light. "Do you see that?"

He stopped beside her, following her line of sight. His eyes widened as he, too, spotted the glow near the summit, nestled against the mountain's peak. "That... it must be the Heartstone."

Freya nodded, her voice filled with a quiet awe. "I never imagined it would look like this. I thought... I thought it would be cold, like the mountain. But it's warm."

Tarek tilted his head, his gaze thoughtful as he took in the distant light. "Maybe it's meant to reflect what we bring to it," he said softly. "For those who seek power, maybe it's cold. But for those who seek... something else, something true... maybe it becomes a beacon."

Freya looked at him, a faint smile playing at her lips. "A beacon of hope."

Tarek returned her gaze, a warmth in his eyes that softened his usual fierceness. "Hope and danger. You can't have one without the other up here."

They stood together in silence, both of them captivated by the light at the summit, the Heartstone's glow casting faint shadows along the mountain path, illuminating their way forward. Freya felt a surge of determination, her recent doubts and fears fading in the face of that steady, pulsing light.

"Tarek," she began, her voice steady but contemplative, "do you think… this place, the Heartstone… do you think it will test us? Beyond what we've faced so far?"

He nodded slowly, his voice filled with a quiet certainty. "I think so. The mountain has already demanded so much from us. But the Heartstone… if it's truly the mountain's core, it may demand something we haven't even imagined."

She swallowed, her fingers gripping the cold rock beneath her as if grounding herself. "But we're prepared. Whatever it asks, we'll face it together."

He smiled, a hint of his usual confidence returning. "That's what makes it different this time. We're not climbing alone. And no matter what it demands… I trust us."

They fell into silence again, the weight of his words settling between them like a comforting warmth. Freya felt a profound sense of calm, something deeper than the rush of victory or the fire of defiance. This was something solid, grounding her as the Heartstone's light guided them higher.

"Do you think it's alive?" Freya asked quietly, her gaze still fixed on the glow.

Tarek raised an eyebrow. "The mountain?"

"The Heartstone," she clarified, her voice a reverent murmur. "It feels… like it's watching us. Like it knows we're coming."

Tarek considered this, his tone thoughtful. "Maybe it is, in a way. Maybe it holds the memories, the essence of those who have come before. Maybe the Heartstone has a will of its own."

Freya's eyes narrowed as she studied the light. "Then it already knows why we're here, what we're prepared to give. And I think…" She hesitated, her voice softening, "I think it may already know us, more than we know ourselves."

Tarek nodded, his voice equally quiet. "Then it's not just the Heartstone we're facing. We're facing our own intentions, our own… truths. Whatever it is we carry, Freya, I have a feeling it'll demand everything."

She looked back at him, a flicker of determination in her gaze. "Then we give it everything. There's no room for fear anymore, no room for second-guessing. If this is the final step, we take it wholeheartedly."

Tarek's expression softened, a mixture of pride and understanding in his eyes. "And we'll face it together, just like we vowed. No hesitation."

Freya gave him a firm nod, her resolve strengthening as they shared one last look at the Heartstone's distant light, glowing like a star against the dark sky. They resumed their climb, their footsteps in sync, each step bringing them closer to the summit, to the culmination of everything they'd fought for, and to the final trial that awaited.

And as they ascended, the Heartstone's light grew brighter, its warmth radiating through the cold, a steady beacon of both promise and challenge. They moved toward it, no longer just travelers on the mountain, but partners bound by something deeper, something destined—ready to face the heart of the mountain, and whatever it held for them, together.

Chapter 12
The Toll of Power

The air was thick with a heavy silence, broken only by the crunch of their boots on the frost-bitten ground. Freya could feel it—the energy draining from her, leaving her limbs heavier with each step. Every pulse of the mountain's cold magic seemed to sap her strength, dulling the edges of her abilities in a way that was both bewildering and infuriating. She glanced over at Tarek, who walked beside her, his face drawn and pale, his breathing uneven.

Tarek met her gaze, his eyes narrowing. "Freya... is it just me, or is something... wrong here? I can barely keep my focus, let alone sense anything with the accuracy I'm used to."

She nodded, gritting her teeth as she struggled to maintain her composure. "It's not just you. The mountain... it's dampening us somehow. I can feel it sapping my energy, more with every step we take." Her voice was low, edged with frustration. "It's like it's testing us, like it's... aware of us."

He scoffed, trying to mask the tension in his voice. "Awareness? You think the mountain is... alive?"

Freya glanced around, her gaze cautious. "In some way, yes. It has to be. I've felt places that were rich with magic, but this is different. It's as if the mountain's energy is... intentional, like it knows how to make us vulnerable."

Tarek rubbed a hand over his face, his expression tight. "Great. So not only are we fighting exhaustion, but we're up against a mountain that's actively working against us."

Freya managed a faint smile, trying to lighten the gravity of the situation. "Think of it as… a challenge. The mountain is testing our limits."

He snorted, though his voice carried a hint of admiration. "Of course you'd see it that way. Always up for a challenge, aren't you?"

"Do I have a choice?" She replied, raising an eyebrow. "Either I rise to the challenge or…" She glanced down the path, swallowing hard. "Or we don't make it out of here."

He met her gaze, his tone softening. "Then we keep moving. I'll pull my weight if you pull yours. Deal?"

Freya nodded, her gaze steady. "Deal. But if one of us falls, the other doesn't leave them behind. Agreed?"

Tarek hesitated, then gave her a firm nod. "Agreed. Though, to be honest, I'm more worried about you leaving me behind." His smirk was faint, but it was there, flickering through his exhaustion.

She rolled her eyes, though her voice softened. "Don't worry, Firelander. You're not getting rid of me that easily."

They continued forward, each step a new trial. Freya could feel the mountain's energy pressing down on her, heavy and unrelenting. It was as though every breath she took was a battle, every movement a test of her endurance. The weight of her drained powers felt like chains around her ankles, pulling her down, demanding more than she thought she could give.

"Tarek," she murmured, her voice strained, "do you feel… weaker than usual? Like even your strength isn't enough?"

He nodded, swallowing visibly. "More than you know. I'm used to heat, not this cold, but it's more than that. It's like something is stripping away what makes me… me."

Freya's eyes darkened. "The mountain is feeding off us. It wants us to rely on nothing but ourselves… our raw strength. It's pushing us to the edge."

He clenched his fists, glancing at her with a determined glint in his eyes. "Then let it push. We're still standing, aren't we?"

A small smile broke through her fatigue. "True enough. But this isn't going to get easier, Tarek. It's only going to get harder the closer we get to the heart of this place."

He took a deep breath, the weariness etched into his face but his resolve unwavering. "I'm ready if you are. Besides… I've got the most stubborn partner on the mountain by my side."

She chuckled, despite herself. "You're not exactly known for backing down either, are you?"

"Not a chance," he replied, his tone fierce. "Let the mountain throw whatever it wants at us. We've come this far, and we're not turning back now."

Freya nodded, feeling a surge of renewed strength as she looked at him. Despite the mountain's draining energy, despite the odds stacked against them, she knew that this was a battle she wouldn't face alone. They were in this together, and that, somehow, was enough.

"Then let's keep going," she said, her voice filled with determination. "No matter what it takes, we'll face it head-on. Together."

The wind cut through them like knives, a bitter reminder of how far they still had to go. Every step seemed to drain what little strength remained, and even Freya, who was used to the mountain's unforgiving elements, felt the weight of exhaustion pressing down. She stole a glance at Tarek, noting the tight lines around his mouth, the way his breath came in labored puffs, clouding the frigid air.

"Doing all right, Firelander?" she asked, trying to keep her tone light, though concern undercut her words.

He met her gaze, his lips pulled into a faint, stubborn smile. "Just… peachy," he said, his voice strained but resolute. "This cold… it's something else. It's like it's trying to steal every bit of warmth I have left."

She frowned, eyeing his thin cloak. "It's not just the cold, Tarek. This mountain's magic is… different. It's sapping our strength, and for you, it's worse. You're not used to this."

He chuckled dryly, his voice barely above a whisper. "Glad you noticed. But don't worry, Freya—I'll keep up."

Freya sighed, a mixture of irritation and admiration filling her as she watched him struggle to steady his breathing. "It's not about keeping up. Look at you. This isn't your world, Tarek, and you're pushing yourself harder than anyone I've ever seen. You have nothing to prove to me."

He looked at her, the hint of a smirk playing on his lips despite his visible exhaustion. "Maybe I do, though. I didn't come all this way to be the weak link."

She rolled her eyes, though a faint smile softened her expression. "Weak link? You're still here, aren't you? Most people wouldn't have made it past the first trial. You're… stronger than I gave you credit for."

Tarek raised an eyebrow, his breath coming in short, quick bursts. "Did I just hear a compliment from Freya, the legendary Guardian?"

"Don't get used to it," she replied, crossing her arms against the biting cold. But the faintest of grins tugged at her mouth. "It's just… surprising, that's all. You're not what I expected."

He tilted his head, his gaze steady. "And what did you expect, exactly?"

She hesitated, her voice softening. "Someone… someone who would give up once it got hard. Someone who wouldn't last in a place like this." She looked away, almost embarrassed. "But you've proven me wrong. Over and over."

He let out a laugh, though it was tinged with weariness. "That's good to know, Freya. Can't have you thinking I'm here just for the adventure."

She glanced back at him, a flicker of respect in her gaze. "I don't, not anymore. You're stronger than you look, Tarek. And I'm not just talking about physical strength."

He seemed taken aback, though he quickly masked it with his usual bravado. "Well, I'll take that as the highest compliment." He grinned, though his expression softened. "But don't forget—you're the one leading us through this. Without you, I'd probably be lost somewhere back on the first pass."

Freya gave a small nod, appreciating the acknowledgment, though she kept her response simple. "That's the idea. We're in this together, remember?"

He met her gaze, and for a moment, the exhaustion in his eyes faded, replaced by something close to admiration. "Together," he repeated, his voice carrying a quiet sincerity that made her heart skip.

They continued in silence for a few moments, each grappling with their own thoughts. Freya broke it, her voice almost hesitant. "You know, I didn't think I'd ever trust someone else to have my back. Not like this."

Tarek looked at her, his gaze softening as he caught the honesty in her words. "Neither did I," he admitted, a rare vulnerability in his tone. "But here we are, somehow still standing… or at least, still moving."

Freya chuckled, her eyes brightening with a touch of warmth. "Let's keep it that way. I think we've both proved we're not the type to give up."

Tarek nodded, determination flashing in his eyes. "Then let's keep moving. This mountain won't know what hit it."

They shared a quiet smile, the bond between them stronger, more certain. The mountain's trials loomed ahead, but they faced it with a mutual respect and a hard-won alliance that, somehow, felt unbreakable.

The wind eased as they stepped into a narrow alcove between two large rock formations, a brief sanctuary from the relentless cold. Freya could feel the bone-deep exhaustion settling over her, and even Tarek, ever resilient, seemed barely able to stand. They sat down on the frozen ground, each leaning heavily against the rock wall, their breaths visible in the chilled air as they took a moment to rest.

Freya broke the silence first, her voice low but edged with a touch of bitterness. "It's like the mountain's intent on draining every last bit of strength from us. My powers are useless out here. It's just… me against this endless cold."

Tarek nodded, rubbing his hands together for warmth. "You're not the only one. My strength feels... hollow, like it's only there until the mountain decides to take it away." He shot a glance at Freya, his eyes dark with frustration. "All my training, everything I thought I could rely on, and here, it's like none of it matters."

She met his gaze, feeling a rare kinship in the vulnerability they shared. "I know what you mean. I spent years honing my skills, thinking there was nothing I couldn't face. And now... it feels like the mountain's mocking me, stripping me down to nothing."

Tarek sighed, leaning back against the rock. "It's more than just survival here, isn't it? It's a test of what we have left when everything else is taken away."

Freya looked over at him, her voice softer, almost thoughtful. "You're right. We're not just fighting the elements. It's as if the mountain wants to see how much we can endure... how far it can push us before we break."

Tarek gave a small, humorless laugh. "If that's the case, it's doing a damn good job of it."

A silence fell over them, heavy and reflective, each of them lost in their own thoughts. Freya's gaze drifted to Eirwen, who sat a few feet away, arms folded, watching them with an expression that bordered on amusement, his face as calm as if he were merely observing a simple exchange.

Freya frowned, her voice laced with suspicion. "Eirwen, you don't seem affected by any of this. While we're practically falling apart, you're… untouched. Not even winded."

Eirwen raised an eyebrow, his lips curving into a faint smile. "The mountain and I have an… understanding," he replied, his tone smooth and cryptic.

Tarek scoffed, his voice tinged with irritation. "An understanding? Care to elaborate on that? Or are we just supposed to believe you're immune to everything this place throws at us?"

Eirwen's gaze flicked between them, a hint of amusement in his eyes. "It's not immunity, Tarek. It's simply… acceptance. I have embraced the mountain's energy, rather than resisting it." He leaned forward slightly, his tone shifting to something almost reverent. "Perhaps you should do the same."

Freya's eyes narrowed, her patience waning. "And what exactly does that mean, Eirwen? Do you know something we don't? Are you holding back information?"

Eirwen shrugged, seemingly unfazed by her sharp tone. "You perceive the mountain's energy as a force against you, an enemy to be fought. But what if you viewed it differently? What if, instead of struggling, you allowed it to reveal what it intends?"

Tarek bristled, his voice laced with defiance. "So we're just supposed to sit here, let it drain us, and wait to see what happens? That's your grand advice?"

Eirwen's calm smile didn't falter. "Think of it not as submission but as harmony. This mountain is ancient, and it demands respect. Sometimes the only way forward is to trust in its guidance, rather than your own strength."

Freya exchanged a look with Tarek, her eyes filled with skepticism. "I don't know if I can trust that. My whole life, I've relied on my strength, my abilities. Relying on something as unpredictable as this mountain… it feels like a trap."

Eirwen regarded her with a steady, unreadable gaze. "Perhaps that's the challenge. To understand that your power, though formidable, is only part of you. The mountain strips that away to reveal who you are without it."

Tarek rolled his eyes, his tone impatient. "Easy for you to say when you're sitting there like the mountain's own chosen emissary. For us, this is survival. And I don't see how embracing exhaustion is going to help us survive."

Eirwen's smile faded slightly, and he studied them both with a cool detachment. "Survival here is as much mental as it is physical. You may have strength, but resilience—true resilience—requires letting go of control. Only then will the mountain allow you to pass."

Freya shook her head, frustration tightening her expression. "I'm not sure I can do that, Eirwen. There's too much at stake. If I let my guard down, if I stop fighting… what's left of me?"

He looked at her with an intensity that bordered on unsettling. "Perhaps that's exactly what you need to discover, Freya."

She held his gaze, feeling a knot of uncertainty tighten in her chest. His words lingered, echoing in her mind, but the idea of surrendering to the mountain's will felt as foreign as the cold itself.

Tarek sighed, rubbing his temples, his voice quieter. "Fine. We'll rest here, as much as we can. But don't expect us to just embrace the mountain's trials with open arms, Eirwen."

Eirwen merely inclined his head, his expression serene. "As you wish. But remember, the mountain has no malice. Only purpose. And it's up to you whether you find meaning in that purpose or resist it."

Freya leaned back, staring into the darkening sky, Eirwen's words swirling through her thoughts. She didn't know if she could ever fully trust his perspective, but for now, they had no choice but to rest, recover, and prepare to face whatever the mountain threw at them next.

The stillness of their shelter offered a brief reprieve, allowing Freya to clear her mind and let the exhaustion ebb, if only slightly. She sat in silence, her back pressed against the cold rock, eyes half-closed as the weight of the journey pressed down on her, grounding her in a way that felt both humbling and empowering. The rest had done her some good; though her muscles still ached and the cold seeped deep into her bones, there was a calm clarity that hadn't been there before.

She looked over at Tarek, who was stirring from his own rest, his eyes opening with a determined glint. Though they had spoken little, the unspoken agreement between them—the promise that they would face whatever came next together—was enough to steady her resolve. Beside him, Eirwen sat motionless, a slight smile playing on his lips as he observed them, his detachment still a reminder of the unknown purpose he carried.

Freya adjusted her gear, her fingers fumbling slightly in the frigid air as she tightened the strap on her cloak and checked her pack. Each movement felt like a ritual, preparing her mind as much as her body. With every hardship the mountain presented, she felt her inner barriers chipping away, leaving her raw but determined. This was not just a test of endurance; it was a trial of spirit. And she knew now, more than ever, that she had to see it through.

She rose to her feet, her gaze shifting between Tarek and Eirwen. "We've rested enough," she said, her voice steady. "Whatever the mountain has planned next, I'm ready."

Tarek grunted as he stood, rolling his shoulders to shake off the lingering stiffness. "It's not like we have much of a choice, right? This place isn't about to let us take it easy." Despite his words, there was a glint of shared purpose in his eyes, a hint of admiration as he looked at her.

Freya managed a faint smile, feeling a flicker of gratitude for his steady presence. "No, it's not. But we've made it this far, haven't we?"

Tarek nodded, his voice laced with a rare softness. "We have. And we're not stopping now."

Her gaze shifted to the misty expanse before them, where the mountain's path twisted into shadow, obscured by an almost tangible presence, as if the mountain itself was waiting. Freya tightened her fists, a quiet resolve settling over her. Each step forward felt like peeling away a part of herself she no longer needed—her doubts, her guilt, her fears. She could feel redemption's pull, distant but steady, drawing her closer with each hardship.

"Every challenge here," she murmured, more to herself than to the others, "is part of the path. Each step, each struggle… it's bringing me closer to what I came here for." Her voice softened, laced with determination. "And I won't let it be in vain."

Eirwen's gaze lingered on her, a quiet satisfaction in his expression. "The mountain knows those who seek its answers sincerely. And it knows those who are prepared to face what it reveals."

She met his gaze, her eyes hard. "I don't care what it reveals, Eirwen. I only care that I finish what I started. I'm not leaving this mountain without the answers I need."

He inclined his head, a faint smile tugging at the corner of his mouth. "Then may the mountain guide you, Freya. Your path is one of purpose, and it's no longer obscured."

She held his gaze for a moment longer, then turned her attention back to Tarek. "Let's move."

Together, they stepped out of the shelter, leaving behind the remnants of their rest and steeling themselves for what lay ahead. The mountain loomed, its presence as foreboding as ever, but Freya's heart was steady. This journey, with all its trials and obstacles, was forging something within her—a strength she hadn't known she possessed, a resilience she had earned through every hardship.

The cold stung her skin, the winds clawed at her cloak, but she walked forward with a fierce resolve. Whatever the mountain had yet to reveal, she would face it head-on, her purpose unwavering.

Chapter 13
The Mountain's Judgment

The narrow pass wound tightly between towering walls of rock, the path no wider than the length of a single stride, forcing them to move one by one, eyes fixed on the treacherous ground. The air grew heavier as they advanced, a strange, charged stillness settling over the mountain, making every sound and movement feel muted, distant. Freya led the way, her senses on high alert as the atmosphere thickened around them, and Tarek followed close behind, his gaze flicking to the looming cliffs above.

Eirwen, bringing up the rear, cleared his throat, breaking the silence. "There's a storm coming," he murmured, his voice a calm ripple in the tense quiet. "But don't expect it to be one of wind or snow."

Freya stopped and turned, her brow knitting as she tried to make sense of his words. "What do you mean? If it's not wind or snow, then what kind of storm are you talking about?"

Eirwen's eyes flickered with a knowing glint, and he offered a faint smile, one that made Freya's skin prickle. "A storm of the mountain's own making. One that doesn't affect the physical world, yet leaves its mark on all who experience it."

Tarek crossed his arms, a skeptical look on his face. "So, what, are we supposed to believe the mountain has some mystical, invisible storm ready to throw at us? This place is harsh enough without vague warnings."

Eirwen didn't respond immediately, his gaze drifting over the cliffs as if he could see something they couldn't. When he finally looked back, his expression was serene, almost reverent. "Believe what you will, Tarek. The mountain has many ways of revealing itself. This storm… it's one of testing, one that will force you to confront what you carry within."

Freya's unease deepened, his cryptic words echoing in her mind. "And how would you know that, Eirwen?" she asked, her tone laced with suspicion. "Have you been through this before?"

Eirwen's faint smile remained, though there was a shadow behind his gaze, a hint of something she couldn't place. "I've witnessed storms like this. They're not meant to harm, but to cleanse… or, perhaps, to reveal."

Freya exchanged a glance with Tarek, feeling her wariness flare. "And yet you seem completely unaffected, as if you know exactly what to expect."

Tarek scowled, his voice edged with irritation. "If you know what's coming, Eirwen, maybe you could stop being cryptic and tell us outright. We've been through enough. I don't have the patience for riddles."

Eirwen's gaze softened, though his detachment never faltered. "Some truths cannot be told outright, Tarek. They have to be experienced, understood through trials. This mountain demands not just strength, but clarity. Facing this storm will bring you closer to that."

Freya clenched her jaw, the discomfort gnawing at her. "So you're testing us, then? Letting us go through whatever this is so we can… what, learn some grand lesson?"

Eirwen tilted his head, regarding her thoughtfully. "It's not I who am testing you, Freya. The mountain has its own will, its own demands. I'm merely here to guide you through what it reveals."

Freya felt a surge of frustration, a tension building within her as she tried to reconcile his words with the calm certainty he projected. "You speak as if the mountain is some kind of living thing," she muttered, half to herself.

"It's alive in its own way," Eirwen replied, his voice quiet, as if sharing a secret. "It knows what lies in the hearts of those who tread its paths. You're here for a reason, Freya, as am I. And the mountain… it recognizes that purpose."

Tarek shook his head, his tone filled with doubt. "Purpose or not, I didn't come here to be judged by a bunch of rocks. I came here to find answers, not get pulled into some mystical trial."

Eirwen's gaze held steady, unbothered by Tarek's skepticism. "Then find your answers, Tarek. But understand, the mountain's challenges aren't just obstacles. They're reflections of what lies within you. If you resist them, you resist yourself."

Freya shifted uncomfortably, his words leaving a strange weight on her mind. She was used to facing external challenges—forces she could fight, obstacles she could overcome through strength and strategy. But an internal storm, a test of her own fears and doubts, was something she hadn't expected.

"Fine," she said finally, her tone firm but wary. "We'll keep going. But if this storm is coming, we'll face it on our terms, not the mountain's."

Eirwen's subtle smile returned, though it held a note of respect. "As you wish, Freya. Just remember, this place has no malice. Only purpose."

They moved forward, the weight of Eirwen's warning pressing down on them as the trail darkened, the air growing thick with an almost palpable energy. Freya's curiosity warred with her distrust, and as they continued, she couldn't shake the feeling that the mountain—like Eirwen—was watching her, testing her resolve in ways she didn't yet understand.

The path narrowed, winding through steep cliffs that loomed on either side, their jagged edges reaching toward a sky thick with gray clouds. Ahead of them, the trail split into two distinct routes: one led up a narrow, rocky incline toward higher ground, while the other descended into a shadowed ravine, disappearing beneath a thick blanket of mist. Eirwen stood at the fork, his gaze drifting between the two paths as he tilted his head, listening to the silence as if it held some hidden message.

Freya and Tarek stopped beside him, exchanging a wary glance. The tension thickened, every second of Eirwen's quiet contemplation adding to Freya's unease. She could feel the weight of the choice before them, the importance of choosing the right path—a choice that Eirwen seemed to be toying with.

Tarek broke the silence, his voice edged with impatience. "What's the holdup, Eirwen? You're the one who knows these paths better than us. Just pick a direction."

Eirwen didn't look at him, his gaze still flickering between the two routes. "The mountain speaks only in whispers," he murmured, as if talking more to himself than to them. "One must listen carefully."

Tarek scoffed, frustration evident in his tone. "More riddles. Either you know where we're going, or you don't. What's it going to be?"

Eirwen finally turned, his gaze calm but thoughtful as he met Tarek's eyes. "Patience, Tarek. The path is not always clear, even to those who have walked it before. The mountain… it shifts, it tests. Sometimes it requires stillness to reveal its intentions."

Freya felt a chill run through her, Eirwen's words settling like a weight on her chest. She watched him, feeling trapped in a strange limbo between his cryptic guidance and the uncertainty of venturing forward alone. Every instinct urged her to keep her distance, to question his motives, yet there was an undeniable pull to follow him—like he was the only bridge between her and the answers she sought.

She cleared her throat, keeping her tone as steady as she could. "So, what exactly are we listening for, Eirwen? The mountain doesn't speak, not in any way we can understand."

He regarded her with an enigmatic smile, his voice soft but unyielding. "You might be surprised, Freya. Sometimes, it's not about understanding in the way we're used to. It's about feeling... intuition. The mountain has its own language, one that requires surrender rather than comprehension."

Freya's jaw tightened, irritation flaring up as she considered his words. "And you expect us to simply trust this... feeling?"

Eirwen nodded, his gaze steady. "Yes. Trust the feeling, trust what the mountain asks of you. Logic and reason will not guide you here; this place requires a different kind of knowing."

Tarek shook his head, his expression filled with doubt. "This is insane. We're putting our lives in the hands of... of whispers and feelings?" He looked at Freya, his voice laced with urgency. "Freya, are you really okay with this?"

Freya hesitated, feeling the pull of Tarek's skepticism but knowing, deep down, that Eirwen held a key to the path she couldn't deny. She took a deep breath, steadying herself. "No, I'm not okay with it. But we have little choice. Eirwen has knowledge we don't. As much as I hate to admit it, we need him to get through this."

Tarek frowned, his expression a mixture of resignation and frustration. "Fine. But if this path turns out to be a trap, I'm holding him accountable."

Eirwen offered a faint smile, unfazed by Tarek's animosity. "As you wish, Tarek. But remember, the mountain will lead us as it sees fit. I am merely a guide, nothing more."

Freya's mind churned, her mistrust bubbling up as she looked at the two paths before them. Every fiber of her being screamed for caution, yet Eirwen's calm certainty made it impossible to turn away. She clenched her fists, feeling the strange conflict within her—reliant on his guidance, yet resentful of how deeply she needed it.

"All right," she said finally, her voice firm but laced with skepticism. "Lead the way, Eirwen. But know this—I'm following because I have to, not because I trust you."

Eirwen's smile widened, a faint glint in his eyes. "Trust is not required, Freya. Only commitment to the path."

They moved forward, stepping into the misty descent as Eirwen led the way, his form melding with the shadows. Freya felt her mind race, questioning why she felt compelled to follow someone she didn't fully trust, and yet, a part of her knew the answer—she wanted the truth that only he seemed to hold.

The path wound downward, deeper into the mist-laden ravine, each step seeming to pull them further into the mountain's depths. The trail was treacherous, littered with loose stones and slick with a thin layer of ice, forcing Freya and Tarek to move with caution. Yet, as Freya stole glances at Eirwen, her unease grew; while she and Tarek stumbled and fought for each step,

Eirwen moved with an effortless grace, as though he was part of the mountain itself, untouched by the fatigue that pressed so heavily on them.

Freya's breathing grew labored, her muscles aching from the unrelenting journey. She grit her teeth, frustrated not only with the physical strain but with the calm, almost serene expression Eirwen wore as he led them onward. His steps were light, his breath even, as if he were merely taking a leisurely stroll. She felt a flicker of suspicion gnaw at her, her mind racing with questions she couldn't quite answer.

She fell back slightly, sidling closer to Tarek. "Does it not bother you?" she murmured, her voice low enough that Eirwen couldn't overhear. "The way he moves, like this mountain has no effect on him?"

Tarek's gaze flickered toward Eirwen, his expression hardening. "You think I haven't noticed? I've been watching him ever since we started this climb. It's like he's drawing strength from somewhere else." He paused, his voice dropping lower. "Or something."

Freya nodded, her voice edged with frustration. "That's what I've been thinking. It's as if he's… connected to this place in a way we can't understand. Almost like he's feeding off it somehow."

Tarek let out a quiet huff, glancing back at Eirwen, who seemed unaware of their exchange. "Trust me, Freya, I don't like it any more than you do. But we're too far in now. Even if we wanted to go back, we wouldn't make it without him. Not through these paths."

Freya clenched her fists, the conflicting emotions twisting within her. She knew Tarek was right; their alliance with Eirwen, tenuous as it was, had become their only path forward. But the thought of relying on someone whose motives remained a mystery made her skin prickle with unease. "I know we need him," she admitted quietly. "But that doesn't make it any easier."

Tarek gave her a grim nod, his voice soft but resolute. "Then we'll just have to keep our guard up. Use him to get through this mountain, and watch his every move."

Freya forced herself to look ahead, her gaze landing on Eirwen's back as he led them, still seemingly untouched by the strain. "Agreed," she murmured, her voice barely audible. "But I won't rest until I know why he's really here."

The path continued to narrow, the mist closing in around them like a thick, tangible presence, making the air feel heavier, colder. Freya felt the chill seep deeper into her bones, her breaths coming in visible puffs, and she fought to keep up with Eirwen's relentless pace. Each step seemed to weigh more, each moment testing her endurance, and yet Eirwen moved on without pause, an inscrutable figure leading them deeper into the unknown.

Her mind churned, the doubt gnawing at her resolve. She wanted to believe that this journey had a purpose, that their struggles were leading them closer to the answers she sought, but Eirwen's calm detachment left her questioning. Every glance at him reminded her of how little she understood about his intentions, and the suspicion grew, clawing at her determination.

Still, she pressed on, her eyes fixed on Eirwen as if by watching him, she might finally unravel the truth behind his motives.

The path narrowed as it climbed, cutting along a sheer cliff that dropped sharply on one side into mist-covered depths. Freya, Tarek, and Eirwen emerged onto a precarious ridge, their steps slowing as the ridge broadened slightly, revealing an expansive view of the mountain stretching upward. Above them, the summit loomed, shrouded in an otherworldly glow that seemed to pulse softly, casting an ethereal light across the craggy rocks. Freya squinted, captivated by the strange radiance, feeling as though the mountain's very essence was concentrated at its peak.

Eirwen stopped, his eyes fixed on the summit, his face softened by an unfamiliar vulnerability. He stood in silence for a long moment, and Freya sensed that something significant was stirring within him. She exchanged a glance with Tarek, her curiosity mounting alongside her ever-present distrust.

Finally, Eirwen spoke, his voice quiet and laced with an emotion she hadn't heard from him before. "I didn't come here merely as a guide," he admitted, his eyes still on the summit.

"This journey isn't just for you or the mountain. I, too, seek something here… something I lost long ago."

Freya felt a chill that had nothing to do with the cold. "What do you mean?" she asked cautiously, searching his expression for any trace of deception.

Eirwen's gaze remained steady, his face etched with a distant sorrow. "A long time ago, I made a choice… one I've regretted ever since. The mountain calls to those in need of redemption, and I am no exception. This path we walk is as much mine as it is yours."

Tarek's expression was a mixture of surprise and skepticism. "Redemption?" he echoed, his tone edged with doubt. "And yet you've been leading us forward like it's all some grand test. Why tell us this now?"

Eirwen let out a slow breath, his gaze shifting from the summit to Freya and Tarek. "Because," he replied, his voice soft but resolute, "the mountain's trials are not merely obstacles. They are reflections, asking each of us to face our pasts, to understand our true selves." His lips quirked into a faint, almost sad smile. "Redemption is not a path one walks alone."

Freya's eyes narrowed, suspicion lacing her gaze. "So you expect us to believe you're on this journey for the same reasons we are? To atone for a mistake?" Her tone was skeptical, her mind racing as she tried to parse the truth from his words.

Eirwen's smile widened, but it held no malice. Instead, there was a strange acceptance in his expression, as if he had anticipated her doubt. "I do not expect you to believe anything, Freya. I know that trust is not easily given." He paused, the faintest hint of vulnerability flickering in his eyes. "But yes, I seek to correct what I have done. And this journey… it is my only chance to do so."

Freya exchanged a glance with Tarek, whose face was drawn with equal parts curiosity and suspicion. She couldn't shake the feeling that Eirwen's words, though earnest, hid something deeper. "If redemption is what you're after, why not tell us sooner?" she pressed, her voice firm. "Why the mystery, the cryptic guidance?"

Eirwen's gaze softened, though the guardedness in his expression remained. "Because the journey requires you to find your own answers, Freya. I am here to help, but only to a point. Each of you must confront what lies within on your own. My role is merely to guide you to that place."

Freya felt a tension settle in her chest, his response doing little to assuage her doubts. "You speak in riddles, Eirwen. Even now, when you claim to share your motives, it feels like there's more you're not telling us."

Eirwen inclined his head slightly, acknowledging her distrust. "Perhaps there is. Or perhaps some truths are only revealed when the time is right." His gaze returned to the summit, his eyes reflective. "The mountain knows when one is ready."

Freya's unease deepened, and she couldn't shake the feeling that Eirwen's presence, though seemingly benign, was tied to something beyond her understanding. Was he merely another traveler seeking redemption, or was he part of a larger, more complex trial the mountain had set for her?

Tarek's voice broke the silence, his tone resigned. "Well, whatever you're hiding, it's too late to turn back now. We're in this together, like it or not."

Freya gave a slow nod, her gaze shifting between Eirwen and the summit's glow. "Yes… together." But the word felt hollow, and her resolve hardened as she turned back to the path. She would follow Eirwen, but she would keep her guard up, determined to uncover the full truth of his motives.

As they pressed onward, the glow from the summit grew brighter, casting an otherworldly light on the trail ahead. Freya steeled herself, knowing that whatever lay beyond this ridge would bring her closer to the answers she sought—and perhaps, to understanding Eirwen's true purpose.

Chapter 14
The Trial of Sacrifice

Freya and Tarek stood before the Heartstone, its radiant light flickering in response to their presence, almost as if it could sense the gravity of their choice. They were silent for a moment, letting the weight of it settle, feeling the deep resonance of the Heartstone's call to them both. Then, without another word, Tarek reached for her hand, intertwining his fingers with hers. His touch was steady, grounding, and Freya found herself drawing strength from it, just as she always had.

Tarek looked at her, his voice low, carrying the weight of all they had endured together. "Are you ready, Freya?"

She met his gaze, her eyes filled with resolve and something softer, something more vulnerable that she had never let anyone else see. "With you? Always."

The Heartstone flared, a warm, golden light filling the summit, casting long shadows around them. Tarek took a deep breath, glancing at their joined hands, his voice tinged with a solemn pride. "You've been my strength, Freya. From the moment we started this journey, you've given me something I thought I'd lost. I… I wouldn't be here without you."

Freya squeezed his hand, her voice soft but steady. "And you've shown me what it means to trust again, to fight for something beyond duty. You're the one who helped me see that there was more to life than just survival. I didn't think I could… care for anyone like this."

Tarek smiled, a faint glimmer of sadness in his eyes. "Then let's seal this, here and now. Whatever the Heartstone demands, we face it as one. We pour everything we are into it, and let it carry our love, our bond, into the world."

She nodded, her gaze unyielding. "Together."

They turned to face the Heartstone, its pulsing light filling the air with an energy that vibrated through their bones. Tarek raised his free hand, the familiar warmth of his fire flaring to life at his fingertips, crackling with intensity. Freya mirrored him, summoning her own ice, the cool, crystalline tendrils forming around her hand, wrapping her in a shimmering aura.

With a shared look, they lifted their hands toward the Heartstone, their powers swirling and merging, fire and ice intertwining in a dance that reflected the unity they had forged. Freya could feel the pull of the Heartstone, drawing on the energy of their elements, its light intensifying as it absorbed their combined strength.

Tarek's voice was barely a whisper, filled with awe. "Freya, do you feel that? It's... it's like it's alive."

She nodded, her gaze fixed on the Heartstone, mesmerized by its glow. "It's as if it's acknowledging us, recognizing our bond."

He turned to her, his eyes soft. "Then let it hold a piece of us, Freya. A piece of what we are, together."

Freya's voice caught, her words laced with both sadness and pride. "Tarek... this is more than just a sacrifice, isn't it? It's... it's us leaving something of ourselves behind."

He smiled, a bittersweet expression on his face. "Then let it be our legacy. A testament to what we found here."

She closed her eyes, her heart filled with a fierce, unbreakable love. "For the realms... and for us."

Their powers surged forward, a final, breathtaking release of fire and ice, swirling around the Heartstone, filling it with a brilliant, blinding light that pulsed with the depth of their emotions. Freya could feel her own energy fading, melding with the Heartstone, but there was no fear—only a profound sense of peace, of completion.

As their powers settled, Tarek's voice, soft and trembling, broke the silence. "Freya... if this is all we have, then... then know that I—"

She met his gaze, her eyes shining with unshed tears. "I know, Tarek. I feel it. And I... I love you, too."

The Heartstone's light flared once more, bathing them in a warmth that felt like an embrace, holding the weight of their sacrifice, sealing their love and their power within its eternal glow. They stood, hands clasped, their hearts steady, knowing that whatever came next, they had given everything. And together, they would always be a part of the mountain, a part of the Heartstone, a beacon for those who would come after.

As the Heartstone absorbed the full force of their powers, its light grew blinding, radiating with a fierce intensity that seemed to pulse in time with their very heartbeats. Freya felt her energy slipping away, the cool, familiar sensation of her ice receding, as if it were being drawn from the depths of her soul. Tarek was beside her, his fire dimming, the warmth flickering, until even his strength waned under the Heartstone's pull.

He staggered slightly, clutching her hand tighter. "Freya, it's… it's taking everything."

Freya nodded, her voice soft, though it trembled with the weight of what they were giving. "It's as if the Heartstone… is asking for more than just our power. It's… it's taking part of us."

Tarek met her gaze, his expression filled with a strange, quiet acceptance. "Then let it. If it means peace, if it means we've done our part, then let it have whatever it needs."

She closed her eyes, feeling the warmth of his hand anchoring her even as her strength ebbed away. "I never thought I'd feel like this," she murmured, her voice barely a whisper. "Like there's a piece of me that can finally rest."

Tarek chuckled softly, though his voice was faint. "I know what you mean. I've spent so long running, trying to be something, someone… and now, standing here with you… I finally feel whole."

The Heartstone's light surged again, and this time Freya felt a pang deep within her, a final tug that nearly brought her to her knees. She clung to Tarek, her voice thick with emotion. "It's... it's almost over, isn't it? Our magic... it's leaving us."

He nodded, his gaze steady, though his eyes held a glimmer of sadness. "Yes. But Freya, we're leaving something behind, something far more powerful. We're giving them hope. Isn't that worth it?"

She looked up at him, the corners of her lips lifting in a small, tender smile. "With you, Tarek, it's worth everything."

He squeezed her hand, his voice growing faint as the last of his fire dimmed, flickering out like a dying ember. "Then let's go together, Freya. Let's give them a light that will last."

The Heartstone pulsed once more, a final, brilliant surge of light that consumed their powers entirely, draining them to the core. Freya could feel the emptiness left in the wake of her magic, a quiet void where once her ice had thrummed with life. Her body felt weak, unsteady, but within that emptiness, there was peace, a profound fulfillment that filled the spaces where her power once resided.

As the Heartstone's light receded, leaving only a gentle glow, Tarek slumped against her, his face pale but peaceful. "Freya... we did it," he whispered, his voice barely audible.

She wrapped her arms around him, pulling him close, her own voice thick with a mixture of exhaustion and pride. "Yes. We did. And look—the Heartstone's glow… it's calm now. Balanced."

Tarek managed a faint smile, his head leaning against hers. "Then it was worth every ounce of power we gave. They'll remember us, Freya. Maybe not our names, but what we did here. And maybe… maybe that's enough."

She nodded, feeling her own strength fading, her limbs heavy but her spirit light. "We've given them a future, Tarek. A chance for peace, for balance. And we did it together."

He lifted his head slightly, his gaze warm, though his exhaustion was evident. "Thank you, Freya. For everything. For standing beside me… even when I didn't deserve it."

Her hand found his, their fingers interlaced, her voice a soft murmur. "You deserved every step, Tarek. You taught me to trust, to open my heart again. For that, I'll always be grateful."

They stood together in the Heartstone's softened glow, the mountain's silence wrapping around them like a final embrace. Freya felt her knees begin to buckle, and she leaned into him, both of them supporting each other as the last remnants of their strength ebbed away. But in that moment, she felt no fear, no sorrow—only the quiet joy of having shared this journey with him.

Tarek's voice, faint but filled with contentment, broke the silence. "We did it, Freya. And whatever happens next… I wouldn't trade this for anything."

She closed her eyes, letting his words settle within her, a warm, comforting presence that filled her with a sense of belonging she had never known. "Neither would I, Tarek. We gave them our all."

They stood there in silence, the Heartstone's light reflecting their sacrifice, their love, and their unity—a legacy forged not from power or ambition, but from the simple, profound choice to trust and to give. And as the mountain's quiet settled around them, they knew that they had fulfilled the Heartstone's demand in the truest, most enduring way possible.

The summit was bathed in the soft glow of the Heartstone, its steady light warm and quiet, like the slow, peaceful breaths of a sleeping giant. Freya and Tarek sat on the ground, leaning against each other, feeling a stillness that neither had experienced in years. Their magic, once so alive and tumultuous within them, had gone silent, leaving an unexpected lightness in its wake.

Freya sighed, her voice gentle as she looked down at her hands, now still and empty. "It's strange, Tarek. All this time, I thought my power was what made me strong. That without it… I'd be nothing."

Tarek smiled faintly, watching her, his own hands resting loosely at his sides. "I know exactly what you mean. It's like… I spent so long defining myself by my fire, by the heat, by the strength it gave me. But now that it's gone, I feel like I can finally breathe. Like I don't have to prove anything."

She looked up at him, her gaze soft and reflective. "You were never defined by your power, Tarek. Not to me. It was your strength, yes, but it wasn't... you."

He chuckled, shaking his head. "Funny. I could say the same about you. I think... I always admired you because you held your power like it was a responsibility, not a weapon. I learned a lot just by watching you."

Freya tilted her head, a hint of a smile tugging at her lips. "And yet you've spent all this time thinking you needed fire to be strong?"

He shrugged, a playful glint in his eye. "Maybe it was habit. Hard to break after so long. But now... now I feel like I'm finally free of it."

She glanced back at the Heartstone, its light reflecting the unspoken words between them. "It's almost like... it took a piece of us, but gave something back. Something we didn't even know we needed."

Tarek's voice softened, thoughtful. "Peace. That's what it feels like. Like I don't have to carry that weight anymore."

Freya nodded, her gaze distant. "For so long, I thought that power was my purpose. But maybe it was only ever meant to be a part of the journey, not the destination."

He reached over, gently taking her hand, his voice steady. "Then what now? What does life look like, Freya, without the ice and fire?"

She squeezed his hand, her smile growing a bit more certain. "Maybe it looks a lot simpler. Maybe it's just... being here, together, facing the world as it is, without the need to control it."

He laughed, his tone warm, a hint of relief shining in his eyes. "Simple sounds perfect. And after everything, I think it's what I've wanted all along. Just... a life where we aren't bound by what we are, but by who we choose to be."

Freya's voice was barely a whisper, filled with a soft, lingering awe. "And we can choose that now, can't we?"

Tarek nodded, a peaceful smile spreading across his face. "Yes. We can finally choose. No more destiny, no more demands. Just... us."

They sat in silence, the weight of his words settling between them, a silent promise, a new beginning. Freya felt her heart beat steady, unburdened, free from the tumult of power, and she realized that for the first time, she could live without wondering if she was enough on her own. Because now, she had Tarek beside her, and together, they were more than enough.

She turned to him, her voice filled with quiet wonder. "Thank you, Tarek. For all of it. For showing me I didn't have to carry everything alone."

He looked at her, his gaze filled with warmth, his voice as gentle as the mountain's stillness around them. "And thank you,

Freya. For making me believe that letting go doesn't mean losing anything."

Their hands remained clasped as they sat before the Heartstone, the echo of their former powers a distant memory, leaving only peace. And as the mountain held its silent vigil over them, Freya and Tarek felt the promise of a life unburdened, a journey yet to come—one they would choose, together, with every step forward.

The mountain had transformed. Where fierce winds and relentless storms once roared, silence and calm now reigned, as if the entire peak had drawn a breath and released it, letting go of the tension that had held it for so long. Freya and Tarek stood at the summit for a final moment, gazing out over the snow-laden cliffs, feeling the weight of the mountain's stillness settle around them, solid and steady.

Freya looked up, her voice quiet but filled with awe. "It's as if… the mountain is at peace now. Do you feel it, Tarek?"

He nodded, his gaze sweeping across the vast, snow-dusted landscape. "I do. It's like the storms weren't just weather—they were a reflection of everything this place was holding, all the power and tension we brought here. And now…" He trailed off, a small, contented smile playing at his lips. "Now it's finally at rest."

They began their descent, each step lighter than it had been on the way up. The snow beneath their boots felt firm but forgiving, the icy ground no longer treacherous but familiar, welcoming. Freya felt the air around her, clear and open, a reflection of the lightness within her. She glanced at Tarek, whose steady, peaceful expression mirrored her own, and smiled.

"It's strange, Tarek. After everything… I thought I'd feel empty without my powers. But I don't." She paused, looking at her hands, as though seeing them for the first time. "Instead, I feel… whole. Like this is who I was always meant to be."

Tarek looked over, his voice soft with understanding. "It's like we finally shed a weight we never knew we were carrying. The power, the duty—it was always a part of us, but it wasn't all of us." He took a deep breath, savoring the crisp mountain air. "Maybe that's what the Heartstone wanted all along—for us to see ourselves beyond what we could do, to understand who we are without it."

She nodded, her eyes shining with a quiet gratitude. "Then it feels right to leave a part of ourselves here, within the mountain, as a memory, a promise to protect the balance. Knowing it's here, holding our sacrifice—it's comforting."

As they continued down, the mountain began to open up to them, paths emerging where there had once been harsh, narrow ledges. The clouds parted, revealing a clear sky, the sun casting a warm glow over the snow-covered peaks. Freya felt a sense of renewal in the light, the mountain's serenity mirroring her own newfound peace.

After a while, Tarek stopped, turning back to gaze up at the summit, his expression contemplative. "It's hard to believe that just a day ago, we were fighting for our lives, facing storms and shadows. Now, it's like a different world up there."

Freya followed his gaze, her voice thoughtful. "It's because we changed. We became something more than just two people on a journey. We became part of the mountain, part of the balance." She smiled, glancing at him. "And we did it together."

He nodded, his hand reaching out to grasp hers. "I wouldn't have it any other way, Freya."

They continued in comfortable silence, the mountain's tranquility wrapping around them like an embrace. The path felt familiar now, each turn, each step aligned with a purpose beyond duty or power. They were no longer climbing to prove themselves, nor were they descending with a sense of loss. Instead, they walked with a quiet fulfillment, knowing that the mountain had been changed by their sacrifice, just as they had been changed by its demands.

As they neared the base, Freya turned, casting one last look at the summit, a soft smile on her lips. "Goodbye, Heartstone," she whispered, her voice carrying through the still air. "Thank you."

Beside her, Tarek murmured his own farewell, his expression filled with gratitude and a sense of finality. "May your peace last, mountain. You hold a part of us now."

They resumed their descent, the mountain's calm echoing in their hearts, each step forward a testament to the peace they had found—peace with themselves, with each other, and with the power they had left behind.

Chapter 15
Acceptance at the Summit

The final ascent loomed before them, a steep, jagged trail winding up the face of the mountain, the summit barely visible through the thin, shifting mist. Freya's breath came in shallow bursts, every muscle in her body protesting with each step, yet she pushed forward, drawn by a mixture of exhaustion and fierce determination. The air around them had grown heavier, charged with a palpable sense of anticipation, as if the mountain itself awaited their arrival, watching, judging.

Tarek walked beside her, his face etched with strain, but his pace never faltered. He glanced over at her, offering a faint smile, one that spoke of shared hardship and quiet strength. "How are you holding up?" he asked, his voice softer than usual, tinged with something almost reverent as they neared the summit.

Freya managed a weak smile, brushing a strand of hair from her face. "Better than I'd expected… but barely." She paused, her gaze fixed on the trail ahead, her voice thick with unspoken emotion. "I keep feeling like every step is being weighed… like the mountain is watching me, waiting to see if I'm worthy."

Tarek nodded, his expression somber. "I know what you mean. There's something… different up here. It's like the mountain knows we're near the end, that it's giving us one last test." He hesitated, searching her face. "But you're ready, Freya. I can see it."

She looked down, her voice wavering. "You say that, but… every step closer, I feel the weight of everything I've done, everything I tried to leave behind. I don't know if I'll ever truly be free of it."

Tarek's gaze softened, his tone gentle but firm. "The way I see it, carrying that weight, remembering what you did and still pushing forward—that's what makes you worthy. The past doesn't define you, Freya. It's how you face it that matters."

Freya swallowed, feeling a swell of emotion rise in her chest. "Maybe you're right. But I can't shake the feeling that this place… it's demanding something more than just survival. It's like it's asking me to… accept it all, every mistake, every regret, and find a way to keep going."

Tarek stepped closer, his hand resting briefly on her shoulder. "You're not alone in this. We've faced this journey together, and I trust you, Freya. I've seen your strength. Whatever happens, know that I believe you've earned the right to be here."

She looked up at him, the weight of his words grounding her, reminding her of the bond they had forged through each trial, each shared struggle. "Thank you, Tarek," she murmured, her voice barely above a whisper. "I don't think I could have come this far without you."

He gave her a small, reassuring smile. "Then let's finish this, together."

They continued up the path, the silence around them deepening, broken only by the crunch of their boots on the frozen ground. As they neared the summit, the air grew denser, filled with an almost sacred stillness that seemed to press against Freya's skin, as though the mountain itself was drawing nearer, its presence enveloping them.

Freya's heart pounded, her mind replaying the moments that had led her here—every decision, every sacrifice, every hardship. She felt the familiar pang of regret, the guilt she had tried to bury, resurfacing with each step. But alongside it was something else, a quiet strength she hadn't known she possessed. Every challenge had shaped her, forced her to confront herself in ways she never imagined, and now, here at the threshold of the summit, she felt the faint stirrings of acceptance.

"I came here to atone," she whispered, more to herself than to Tarek, her voice catching in the stillness. "To prove to myself that I was worthy, that I could face what I'd done… and maybe, somehow, leave it behind."

Tarek glanced at her, his expression unreadable. "And now that we're here?"

Freya took a deep breath, feeling the weight of her words. "I don't know if I can ever leave it behind. But maybe… maybe I can carry it differently, not as a burden, but as a part of me. Something that made me who I am."

Tarek nodded, his voice gentle. "That sounds like acceptance to me, Freya. And I think the mountain… it respects that. I know I do."

They stood together in silence, the summit's glow growing brighter, casting long shadows across the ridge as they prepared to take the final steps. Freya felt a profound calm settle over her, a quiet resolve that softened the edges of her guilt, her regret. For the first time, she felt as though she could face her past without being consumed by it, could hold her memories with compassion rather than judgment.

"Let's go," she said, her voice steady, filled with a new determination. Together, they stepped toward the summit, the air around them thick with the promise of absolution and the weight of everything they had faced.

As they neared the summit, Freya felt the mountain's silent judgment ease, as if it, too, recognized the strength she had gained—the strength to accept herself, fully and without fear. And as they crossed the final threshold, she knew that whatever lay ahead, she would meet it with the unwavering resolve born of every step that had brought her here.

As they reached the summit's edge, the mountain stretched out before them, vast and endless, bathed in a soft, ethereal glow. Freya felt an overwhelming stillness settle around her, the weight of her journey pressing down as she took in the sight. She moved a few paces ahead of Tarek, her gaze focused on the mist that seemed to swirl around the edges of the peak, thickening, almost as if it were alive.

Then, from within the mist, a figure emerged—tall, cloaked, and unmistakably familiar. Freya's heart stopped, her breath caught in her throat as Elder Iska appeared before her, his form more vivid than any vision she had encountered. He stood silent, his eyes piercing, and Freya felt as though he were seeing into her very soul. His gaze was a mixture of sorrow and pride, a look that sent a shiver through her.

"Freya," he began, his voice soft yet resonant, a sound she had longed to hear since her exile. "You have come far."

Freya's voice was barely a whisper, choked with emotion. "Elder Iska... is it really you?"

Iska gave a slow nod, his expression unwavering. "In spirit, if not in flesh. I am here because you have reached the edge of your path... and there are questions yet to be answered."

Freya's gaze dropped, her throat tightening as memories of her past flooded back—the choices she had made, the actions that had led to her exile. "I've come seeking redemption," she said, her voice trembling. "To atone for what I did, to prove that I can still be the Guardian I once was... the Guardian you trained me to be."

Elder Iska's face softened, but his eyes held a flicker of doubt. "You were once my most promising pupil, Freya. But power and pride are a dangerous mix. Have you truly learned from your exile, or is this journey simply a means to reclaim what you lost?"

Freya looked away, feeling the weight of his words sink into her. "I… I know I made mistakes. I thought I was protecting our people, but I ignored the counsel of those wiser than me. My pride led me astray, and I've paid the price." She paused, her voice thick with regret. "I've been through hardships, faced trials that I never imagined. And they have shown me… how much I still have to learn, how much I owe to those I left behind."

Elder Iska regarded her, his gaze both stern and compassionate. "Acknowledging your mistakes is the first step, Freya. But being a Guardian requires more than repentance. It demands humility, patience, and a dedication to the balance we are sworn to protect."

Freya's fists clenched as she forced herself to meet his gaze. "I understand that now, Elder. This journey… it has stripped me down to my core, forced me to confront the parts of myself I wanted to ignore. I may never be able to undo the past, but I can choose what I become from here forward. I won't let my past define me."

A faint smile appeared on Iska's face, the pride in his eyes clear, though tempered by caution. "You have changed, Freya. I can see that. But are you prepared to carry the weight of the Guardian's mantle once more, knowing that it will test you again and again?"

Freya nodded, though her voice wavered. "Yes. I'm ready to face whatever comes next. I may still carry the guilt, but I've come to accept it as part of me. It's a reminder of where I went wrong, and where I can choose to go now."

Elder Iska's expression softened, his voice carrying a quiet warmth. "Then you have taken the first steps toward redemption, Freya. Remember, the journey of a Guardian is never easy, and forgiveness is not a single act but a lifetime of choices. Continue as you have, and one day you may find the peace you seek."

Freya's vision blurred, tears stinging her eyes as she took a step closer, reaching out instinctively. "Elder Iska… I'm so sorry for the pain I caused. I didn't realize… I couldn't see…"

Iska raised a hand, his smile gentle as he interrupted her. "The past is a teacher, Freya, not a prison. Remember what you have learned here. Hold your purpose close, and let it guide you. I am proud of you, my child."

As his words settled over her, Elder Iska's form began to fade, dissolving into the soft mist surrounding the summit. Freya watched, feeling a sense of peace wash over her, as if a weight she had carried for so long had finally been lifted. The regret and shame that had haunted her felt quieter, replaced by a calm resolve.

Tarek stepped forward, his voice low but filled with respect. "Freya… are you all right?"

She turned to him, a faint but genuine smile on her face. "Yes, Tarek. For the first time in a long time… I think I am." She glanced back to where Elder Iska's spirit had stood, her heart full with the knowledge that she could move forward—stronger, wiser, and with the courage to face the future, wherever it might lead.

The summit had grown still, a serene silence settling over Freya and Tarek as they processed the vision of Elder Iska and the sense of peace it had left in its wake. Freya felt lighter than she had in years, a calm resolve filling her as she looked out over the vast, mist-covered expanse of the mountain. But just as she took a deep breath, savoring the clarity, a sudden, chilling gust of wind tore through the summit, colder than anything she'd felt before.

The force of it knocked her back, and she stumbled, feeling the biting cold cut through her layers. Tarek, too, was thrown off balance, his hand instinctively reaching for his weapon as he steadied himself. The wind howled, swirling with an unnatural energy, and a dark shape began to form within the mist, towering and ethereal, its presence filled with a raw, ancient power. Freya's heart raced as the figure took shape—a spectral guardian, an imposing creature bound to the mountain, its form shifting and flickering like the shadows cast by flames.

Tarek's voice was tense, barely above a whisper. "Freya… what is that?"

She swallowed, gripping her weapon tightly. "An ancient guardian… a final test." Her voice was filled with both awe and dread. "I think it's here to judge us… to see if we're truly worthy."

The creature's eyes burned like cold embers as it fixed its gaze upon them, a silent, powerful judgment radiating from its form. Without warning, it lunged, its spectral claws slashing through the air, and Freya and Tarek barely had time to dodge. Tarek raised his sword, his voice filled with determination. "Guess we're not getting out of here without a fight!"

Freya moved beside him, her weapon raised as she watched the creature's every move. "Together, then," she replied, and they charged, striking in unison, their weapons passing through the creature's form with little effect, as though it were woven from mist itself.

The guardian's response was swift, a sweeping blow that sent them sprawling across the rocky ground. Freya grunted as she landed, feeling the sting of the cold permeate her body. She pushed herself up, her mind racing. "It's not going to fall from brute force. It's here for something else."

Tarek's jaw was tight as he scrambled to his feet, his breaths visible in the freezing air. "Then what does it want?"

Freya looked into the guardian's glowing eyes, the depths of its ancient gaze seeming to pierce through her. And suddenly, it struck her—the vision of Elder Iska, his words about acceptance and humility, about facing herself fully and without reservation. This was the final test, a trial of her resolve and her willingness to accept herself, mistakes and all.

"It wants… sacrifice," she whispered, lowering her weapon as realization settled over her. "It's not here to test our strength. It's here to see if I'm willing to let go, to trust in something greater than myself."

Tarek's eyes widened. "Freya, you can't just—"

She raised a hand, stopping him. "I have to do this, Tarek." Her voice was calm, resolute. "All my life, I've tried to control my fate, to prove myself through strength. But maybe true strength is in letting go."

She stepped forward, facing the guardian directly, lowering her weapon and meeting its gaze. The creature hesitated, its form wavering, as if uncertain. Freya took a deep breath, her voice steady but filled with conviction. "I accept whatever judgment you pass. I will live by my principles, not for the acceptance of others, but because it's who I am."

The guardian stilled, its eyes fixed upon her, and for a moment, Freya felt a strange calm wash over her, a release of the burden she'd carried. She no longer felt the need to prove herself, to fight against her past. This moment was her truth, her acceptance.

The creature's form softened, its spectral edges dissolving, and Freya saw something almost like respect in its gaze. The guardian inclined its head, acknowledging her growth, and with a final, sweeping gust of wind, its form dissipated, leaving the summit silent once more.

Tarek approached her, his face a mixture of awe and relief. "Freya... that was incredible. You—"

She turned to him, a faint but peaceful smile on her face. "I think I finally understand now, Tarek. This journey wasn't about being forgiven or proving my worth. It was about finding peace with who I am."

He nodded, a look of pride in his eyes. "And you did it. You faced the mountain, and you came out stronger."

Freya took a deep breath, savoring the tranquility that had settled over her. She had confronted her fears, her regrets, and emerged whole, a weight lifted from her heart. As they looked out over the mountain's edge, she knew that, whatever lay ahead, she was ready to face it.

As the last wisps of the guardian's form dissipated into the air, Freya stood still, feeling a profound sense of lightness settle within her. The guilt, the weight of her past mistakes—all of it felt distant, like shadows in the light of dawn. For the first time since her exile, she felt free, her heart unburdened by the relentless need to prove herself. She took a deep, steadying breath, allowing the calm to wash over her.

Tarek stepped forward, his eyes filled with admiration. "Freya... I don't think I've ever seen someone face themselves like that. You faced that guardian without a weapon, without armor. Just… yourself." His voice was almost reverent. "You were incredible."

Freya met his gaze, a warm smile breaking across her face. "I couldn't have done it alone, Tarek. You were there every step of the way. We faced this together."

He chuckled, shaking his head. "Maybe, but you were the one who showed me what it means to keep going, even when everything's stacked against you." He paused, his tone softening. "Thank you… for bringing me along, for showing me that there's more to strength than fighting."

She nodded, feeling the truth of his words resonate within her. "You showed me just as much. Without you, I might have lost hope halfway up that mountain. You reminded me that strength doesn't always mean going it alone."

They stood in comfortable silence, the bond they'd forged on the mountain deepening in those unspoken moments. After a while, Tarek glanced at the vast landscape stretching out before them, his voice filled with wonder. "So, what now, Freya? You've climbed the mountain, faced your past. What comes next?"

Freya's gaze drifted to the horizon, her expression peaceful. "I think… I go back. Back to the world, to wherever the path leads me. I don't need to prove myself to anyone else now. I know who I am, and that's enough."

Tarek nodded thoughtfully, a faint smile playing on his lips. "Then I think I'll be heading my own way too. This journey… it's given me more than I expected. I came looking for answers, and I found something even better—purpose."

She turned to him, her voice quiet. "I'm glad, Tarek. I have no doubt that whatever you choose to do next, you'll do it with the strength and honor I've seen in you."

He laughed, his voice light. "You sound like a Guardian already."

Freya smiled, feeling a warmth in her chest. "Maybe I am, in spirit. I don't need the title anymore to know what I stand for."

They lingered at the summit, gazing over the world below, knowing that this was both an ending and a beginning. After a while, Freya turned to Tarek, extending her hand. "Thank you, Tarek. For everything."

He took her hand, his grip firm but gentle. "Thank you, Freya. For showing me what true resilience looks like."

They stood there a moment longer, hands clasped, before Freya released him, turning toward the descent. With a final nod, they began their separate paths, each carrying the strength they had gained from the mountain.

As Freya moved down the path, she felt a newfound sense of self settle within her, a quiet, steady confidence that had nothing to do with titles or validation. She had faced her demons, her regrets, and emerged whole. She was a Guardian in spirit, ready to carry her truth forward into whatever lay ahead. And as she took each step down the mountain, she knew that, whatever challenges awaited, she would meet them with peace and purpose, her heart light and her resolve unbreakable.

Epilogue
A Guardian Reborn

Freya stood at the foot of the mountain, her gaze tracing the path she and Tarek had forged from its heart. A soft morning light stretched across the landscape, melting away the final remnants of darkness and revealing the world beyond the mountain's cold, harsh grip. For the first time, Freya saw the mountain not as a place of exile but as a silent witness to her transformation.

She turned back for a final look at the peak, feeling a strange sense of kinship with the snow-covered cliffs and icy ledges. What had once felt like a prison now seemed like an old friend, one who had pushed her to her limits and, in doing so, revealed parts of herself she hadn't known existed. She could still feel the weight of Elder Iska's vision, his gentle approval mingling with the mountain's judgment, both of them etched into her memory.

Behind her, Tarek appeared from their small encampment, his steps steady despite the bruises and exhaustion that marked their journey. "Ready to go?" he asked, his voice calm and familiar. They had come to understand each other in those final trials, and Tarek, like her, had faced the mountain's relentless tests and emerged with his own kind of clarity.

Freya met his gaze, a faint smile tugging at her lips. "Yes. I think it's time."

They walked in silence, the dawn breaking over the horizon, bathing them in a warm glow as they descended from the mountain. Freya could feel each step drawing her away from her past—her regrets, her mistakes, her exile—all of it fading into a chapter she could now close. She had thought redemption would be a heavy mantle, a constant reminder of her guilt, but now, she felt it lift from her like a weight left behind on the summit. What remained was something different, something simple and profound: a quiet acceptance of who she was and the power she held within herself.

As they reached the edge of the Rift, Tarek paused, turning to her with a look of genuine respect. "Freya," he began, his voice careful. "I have to say… I didn't think I'd be coming down this mountain with anyone, let alone an Ice Guardian."

She chuckled, warmth in her gaze. "I'm not the Guardian I was, Tarek. The mountain made sure of that."

Tarek nodded, his expression thoughtful. "Maybe that's what it does, then. It takes us apart and rebuilds us… stronger. More aware." He glanced toward the distant lands ahead, his gaze growing distant. "I think… I think we were meant to climb this mountain together. I don't know why, but it feels like part of something larger."

Freya studied him, realizing that he, too, had found purpose in their journey. She extended a hand. "Wherever you go next, Tarek, remember that purpose. Hold on to it."

He clasped her hand firmly, a smile spreading across his face. "And you, Freya. I know that whatever lies ahead, you'll walk your path with honor."

They released their hands, the moment settling between them like a pact, and then, without another word, they went their separate ways—Freya toward the open expanse of her homeland and Tarek toward the lands beyond.

As she walked, her mind drifted back to the heart of the mountain, to the guardian who had tested her resolve. She remembered standing before it, weapon lowered, offering herself fully, stripped of titles and pride. It had been the most vulnerable she had ever felt, yet also the freest. Freya was no longer burdened by the need for validation; she had found her own strength in her willingness to embrace the truth of who she was, flaws and all.

In the days that followed, Freya returned to her village, her steps measured, her heart calm. People looked at her with wonder, and, perhaps, a touch of awe. Whispers circulated, some of disbelief, others of admiration. Her appearance alone—worn but resilient, her gaze steady and calm—spoke volumes. Those who had once looked down on her now regarded her with something akin to respect. She could feel Elder Iska's approval, a warmth within her that grew each time she felt her own resolve strengthen.

Though her journey up the mountain had ended, Freya knew that her true journey had only just begun. The call to be a Guardian was no longer about duty or honor in the eyes of others; it was about the values she had chosen to live by, the strength she had found within herself. She would walk her path with the confidence that had come from her trials, her title of Guardian restored not by the council, but by her own actions and integrity.

Each morning, as she watched the sun rise over the peaks in the distance, Freya would remember the mountain, the journey she had endured, and the redemption she had won. And with each day, she felt a quiet joy growing within her—a joy born not of triumph, but of peace.

In the heart of that peace lay a promise she had made to herself: that she would be the Guardian Elder Iska had believed she could be, not out of obligation, but because it was who she was meant to be. The mountain had stripped her bare, tested her limits, and in the end, left her whole.

Milton Keynes UK
Ingram Content Group UK Ltd.
UKHW041005111124
451035UK00002B/333